Benjamin Gough

Kentish Lyrics, Sacred, Rural, and Miscellaneous

Benjamin Gough

Kentish Lyrics, Sacred, Rural, and Miscellaneous

ISBN/EAN: 9783744788083

Printed in Europe, USA, Canada, Australia, Japan

Cover: Foto ©Andreas Hilbeck / pixelio.de

More available books at **www.hansebooks.com**

KENTISH LYRICS

Sacred, Rural, and Miscellaneous

BY

BENJAMIN GOUGH

AUTHOR OF "LYRA SABBATICA

" Kent, in the commentaries Cæsar writ,
Is termed the civilest place of all this isle :
Sweet is the country, because full of riches ;
The people liberal, valiant, active, wealthy."
SHAKSPEARE.

LONDON

HOULSTON AND WRIGHT

65, PATERNOSTER ROW

MDCCCLXVII.

THIS VOLUME OF

"𝕶𝖊𝖓𝖙𝖎𝖘𝖍 𝕷𝖞𝖗𝖎𝖈𝖘,"

BY HIS LORDSHIP'S PERMISSION,

IS

DEDICATED TO

THE RIGHT HONOURABLE LORD HARRIS,

OF BELMONT, KENT,

AS

AN EXPRESSION OF ESTEEM FOR HIS CHARACTER,

AND THE

NUMEROUS PUBLIC SERVICES

WHICH HE HAS RENDERED TO HIS COUNTRY,

AT HOME AND ABROAD.

PREFACE.

THE favourable reception which has been accorded
to the Author's former Work, "Lyra Sabbatica," both
by the Public and the Press, has induced him to
publish the present Volume.

Most of the poems now presented are of recent
composition, and only a few have been before
printed. They are not, as in the former volume,
exclusively Sacred and Devotional, but the book is
divided into three parts—Sacred, Rural, and Miscellaneous. Of the sacred poems it need only be
said that they are in harmony with Holy Scripture,
and so entirely unsectarian that they may be used
by all sincere Christians.

The second part contains poems on Country life,
and Rural themes, suggested by the ever-renewing
variety and proverbial richness of Kentish scenery,

and by the changing Seasons, so little known or appreciated in cities and towns; but, in all their phases, equally beautiful to such as study and admire Nature as the daily exponent of our Divine Creator's love to His creatures, thus enabling them to look through Nature up to Nature's God.

The third part contains a few Poems on Miscellaneous subjects.

The Author commends the Work to the indulgence of his readers, hoping that the perusal of "Kentish Lyrics" may serve to promote reverential love to God in His Word and in His Works, and inspire a keener thirst and relish for whatever is beautiful and pure and good.

> "When as the pliant Muse, straight turning her about,
> And coming to the land as Medway goeth out,
> Saluting the deare soyle, O famous Kent, quoth she,
> What countrey hath this isle that can compare with thee!
> Which hast within thyselfe as much as thou canst wish,
> Thy conies, venson, fruit, thy sorts of fowle and fish,
> And what with strength comports, thy hay, thy corne, thy wood:
> Not any thing doth want that anywhere is good."
>
> MICHAEL DRAYTON, 1613.

MOUNTFIELD, NEAR FAVERSHAM,
May 15, 1867.

CONTENTS.

PART ONE.—SACRED POEMS.

PART TWO.—RURAL POEMS.

Contents.

xii

Contents.

PART THREE.—MISCELLANEOUS POEMS.

KENTISH LYRICS.

Part One.—Sacred Poems.

MORNING.

WHEN the sweet eyelids of bright morn, awaking
    From night's dark slumbers, open in the east,
And golden flashes of the daylight, breaking,
    Fall upon man and beast ;

Then, as the gentle dews refresh creation,
    The dew of grace refreshes from above ;
And we kneel down in humble adoration
    Before the God we love.

Just as the breath of morning is ascending
    Heavenward on every breeze to God's abode ;
So first, ere yet with men and duty blending,
    I see the face of God.

B

The birds are up, and in full song before us;
  At radiant sunrise they begin their praise,
And break into an universal chorus,
    Which shames our colder lays.

Now will I worship, while the sun's warm beamings
  Shine through my lattice with a welcome smile;
And on my knees—escaping from night's dreamings—
    Prepare for daily toil.

Now will I wait on God in deep devotion,
  Before my anchor for the day I lift;
Lest, in some tempest on life's turbid ocean,
    I from my God should drift.

Now, if God's love perfume my longing heart,
  Fragrant till nightfall shall it still remain;
Duty shall be delight, and day depart,
    Nor leave a sinful stain.

Thus in the royal majesty of life
  Another day I live, but ere I go
Into the battle-field of daily strife,
    My God! Thy grace bestow.

Bowing in reverence and high communion,
  I bathe my soul and wash away my sins
In blood divine; and thus, in hallowed union
    With God, my day begins.

So, with the sanctifying seal celestial
  Stamped on my heart, my daily path is trod;
And through the thorny road of things terrestrial,
    I humbly walk with God.

EVENING.

WELCOME is the gentle hush
  Of evening's silent hour,
Softly fades the sunset flush
  Beneath night's soothing power.
As the whirl of daily strife
  Now subsides in placid rest,
Breathe, O God, Thy peace, Thy life,
  Thyself into my breast.

Through the day Thy guiding hand
  Has kept my soul secure ;
Every step Thy goodness planned
  To make my goings sure.
Thee, my Father and my God,
  I have felt for ever nigh ;
Like a child, my path I trod
  Beneath my Father's eye.

'Mid the crowded haunts of men,
  By pride and evil stirred,
Sweeter far than angel's strain
  Thy loving voice I heard.
" Keep thy heart from sin," it said,
  " And peace and heaven-born joy are thine."
God was near, my present aid,
  And whispered, "Thou art Mine."

Now at eventide I pray,
    And mingle praise with prayer,
Shielded through another day
    By omnipresent care.
Ere I lay me down to rest,
    Speak again, O gracious Lord ;
Make Thy servant doubly blest,
    Who waits to hear Thy word.

Sprinkled with atoning blood,
    And filled with Jesu's love,
Now I sleep and wake with God,
    His conscious presence prove.
Free from dangers and alarms,
    Calmly confident, I sleep
In the everlasting arms,
    While guardian angels keep.

SWEET WORDS TO ME.

TREMBLING penitent, I cried
    For mercy, smiting on my breast.
"Come unto Me," my Lord replied ;
    "Come now, and I will give thee rest."
Sweet words to me ! I heard, I came,
And mercy found through Jesus' name.

Once, sorely tempted by the foe,
    My faltering steps had well-nigh gone,
But Jesus' voice said, "Onward go !
    My strength in weakness I make known."
Sweet words to me ! I grasped His hand,
Enabled thus by faith to stand.

Cast in the furnace next, the flame
    Wreathed round my head with threatening roar;
But soon my great Deliverer came,
    And whispered, "Trust My love and power."
Sweet words to me ! the fiery blast
Nor scorched nor harmed, and soon was past.

Down in affliction's deepest waves
    I sank in waterfloods of grief,
But there a voice said, "Jesus saves,
    His mercy brings thee sure relief !"
Sweet words to me ! affliction fled,
And left me smiling health instead.

Mourning my inbred sin, I prayed,
  "O give me, Lord, a heart renewed."
Again I heard a voice which said,
  "Come to the fountain of My blood!"
Sweet words to me! sweet Saviour too!
My heart was cleansed and formed anew.

Walking at last, when death drew near,
  Through the dark valley's dreaded shade,
"Fear not," said Jesus; "I am here,
  My rod and staff shall be thine aid."
Sweet words to me! for now I sing
In death, "O death, where is thy sting?"

THE WORDS OF JOB.

Job xix. 23—27.

THAT my words were written
    And printed in a book,
Graven on a rock unsmitten,
    Which thunders never shook;
With iron pen recorded
    In words which perish never,
By coming ages hoarded,
    Words made to live for ever !

O Job, thy prayer victorious
    Is answered every day,
In triumphs great and glorious,
    And faith's exulting lay ;
And millions live to cherish
    Thy words of power divine ;—
They live, they cannot perish,
    Those burning words of thine.

Down in the dreary valley
    Full often are they heard ;
And drooping spirits rally,
    With heavenly courage stirred.
Thy voice sweet comfort giveth,
    While victors shout, "I know
That my Redeemer liveth,"
    And conquers every foe.

At the dark grave-side standing,
  That prison-house of gloom,
Where mingled horrors bauding,
  Affright us with our doom,
Thy words of exultation
  Light up e'en death's abode,
And whispers of salvation
  Relieve the mourner's load.

The Judge in pomp descending,
  To gather His elect ;
Stars falling, and graves rending,
  The dead in Christ expect.
When time with age grows hoary
  Thy words shall still remain,
Till Christ shall come in glory,
  In every heart to reign.

O words of life eternal !
  Oh ! when shall I behold
Green pastures ever vernal,
  The city of pure gold ?
Jesu, Redeemer, Brother,—
  Enthroned in heaven's abode,
And mine eyes—not another—
  Gaze on the face of God ?

TO CHRIST'S SOLDIERS.

THE soldier's death is glorious
    Who dies for Jesus fighting,
    In his right hand a flaming brand
      'Midst battle's roar exciting.
Close following his Captain,
    The blood-red banner flying,
The alien's rout and victor's shout
    Are music while he's dying.

The soldiers of Immanuel
    Are sons of God right royal,
Who, leal and true, their strength renew,
    To Jesus always loyal.
They scorn the base deserter,
    Whose craven heart is shaking;
Fresh conquests won, they still go on,
    The strength of Satan shaking.

Fight on, ye brave battalions,
    Till every land and nation
Shall Jesus own, and earth enthrone
    The Captain of salvation.
From conquering to conquer,
    Press on, the war renewing,
Till earth shall sing that Christ is King,
    All saving, all subduing.

Then comes earth's bright millennium,
    Before old time grows hoary;
Sweet love's increase, the reign of peace,
    And Christ in gospel glory.
Peace and good-will for ever,
    And no more sin or sorrow;
Your standard sway, the fight to-day
    Will bring the peace to-morrow.

MARTYRDOM OF JOHN THE BAPTIST.

N Herod's birthday, with a birthday greeting,
   Came lords of high estate ;
And wealth, and might, and peerless beauty
    meeting,
   At Herod's banquet sate.

Bright shone the splendour everywhere surrounding
   Those marble halls,
Blazing with light, while sweetest music sounding,
   Echoed along the walls.

From golden cups the rosy wine was flowing,
   Until men's brows were flushed ;
And songs of softest melody were glowing,
   In strains which charmed and hushed.

Hearts throbbed in rapture, and bright eyes were glancing
   Delight, such joy to prove ;
And see ! the daughter of Herodias dancing,
   Melts Herod into love.

O glorious banquet ! but with tragic ending ;
   Beneath that witching glare,
Incest and lust, and wrath and murder blending,
   Are with Herodias there.

O dreadful banquet ! see Herodias' daughter
    Bearing the sacred head
Of John the Baptist, reeking fresh from slaughter,
    In the warm˜blood just shed !

Silent and lonely, sleeping in his prison,
    He only woke to die !
The headsman struck, and lo ! the martyr risen
    Is glory-crowned on high.

Darkened and dreadful are those halls forsaken,
    The lights are quenched in blood ;
But fiery waves of vengeance have o'ertaken
    The murderers like a flood.

So from that banquet's glittering pavilions
    Voices of warning come,
That men may shun and tremble, and earth's millions
    Escape the sinner's doom.

But from that prison, where the Lord's true servant
    On that dark night was slain,
Calm words are whispered to the ear observant,—
    "The martyr's death is gain ! "

FAITH, HOPE, AND CHARITY.

FAITH grasped the cross, and cried,
  " Here is my trust, in nought beside :
  By this I conquer every foe,
  And on to further victories go.
    Jesus hath died !
Here resting, calmly I defy
  Both earth and hell allied,
And for my dear Lord live or die ! "

Hope joined in full accord,
And sweetly sang of heaven's reward :—
" A pilgrim here I roam,
A pilgrim travelling home ;
  I seek my risen Lord.
Come sorrow, suffering, pain,
  My paradise restored
Of bliss and joy I soon shall gain ! "

Most beauteous of the three,
Love, smiling, said, " Come, follow me ;
And Faith and Hope, refined by Love,
Omnipotent shall prove,
  And gain the victory ! "
So on they went, this loving three,
  Made one by love, God's face to see
And love, to all eternity.

OUTDOOR WORSHIP.

BENEATH heaven's canopy's o'erarching splen-
      dour,
  Cloudless and brilliant with celestial hue,
A silent congregation met to render
    Their worship pure and true.

The preacher stood, with gesture calm and solemn,
  Under the welcome shadow of an oak ;
In his right hand he held the holy volume,
    As in God's name he spoke.

First rose the hymn from many mingled voices,
  Reverent but cheerful, jubilant but sweet,
Acceptable as when heaven's choir rejoices,
    Where saints and angels meet.

Uncovered now, and on the greensward bending,
  The sound of prayer re-echoes through the glen,
Prayer ardent and in faith to heaven ascending,
    Winged with one wide Amen.

Then came the sermon, every glowing sentence
  Flashing with gospel light and sacred power ;
The trumpet-call of sinners to repentance
    In this accepted hour.

Christ's high ambassador entreats, beseeches,
   And pleads with sinners through the covenant blood ;
Vehemently, like noble Paul, he preaches,
      " Be reconciled to God !"

So yielding hearts receive the truth's impression,
   So comes the Spirit as in olden days,
And soon the cry of penitent confession
      Is turned to rapturous praise.

God's own right arm is bared, and showers of blessing
   Come with the word in saving fulness down,
Falling on all, and every heart impressing,
      God's ordinance to crown.

And placid joy succeeds the deep conviction,
   And broken hearts are gently bound and healed ;
Then the doxology and benediction,
      And thus the grace is sealed.

THE WOODLAND CHURCH.

WHOEVER holds communion with the
    skies,
    Will love and reverence God's house
      of prayer,
Where daily praises like sweet incense rise,
    And troubled mourners in their grief repair.

Her glorious bulwarks, and heaven-piercing towers,
    Are dear and sacred to the loving heart,
Where hallowing influence comes down in showers,
    And brightening hopes their welcome joys impart.

But not alone in temples made with hands
    God dwells, but oft in forest wild, and wood ;
From cities far His own cathedral stands,
    And there He communes with the meek and good.

How beautiful, within this lone retreat,
    Amidst these stately rows of oak and birch,
To join in worship, and together meet,
    Beneath the shadow of a woodland church !—

A woodland church, with porch all overgrown,
    Where ivy and clematis interlace,
And garlands of wild roses, newly blown,
    Hang down, festooned in beauty and in grace.

The nave and aisles are marked by pillar-trees,
   Strong and majestic in their girth and height;
Transept and chancel, where the summer breeze
   Whispers of sanctities of love and light.

What art can emulate fair nature's skill?
   See how the roof umbrageous is entwined,
And twisted boughs, and living rafters fill
   The space o'erhead, artistic and refined.

Only in summer comes the human choir
   To sing high praises in this rural fane,
And yearly light afresh its altar fire
   With hymn and chant of high melodious strain.

Unless, perchance, some wanderer in the wood
   Enters alone, and bows in silent prayer,
Unseen of men to ask some heavenly good,
   Or seek deliverance from some earthly care.

But all the year, and every day and night,
   Nature's pure offerings to heaven ascend
In grateful songs, and all her powers unite,
   And all her choristers unceasing blend.

When winter frowns, and storms and tempests rage,
   The choir sonorous with intonings high,
Delights in choral service to engage,
   And swells loud anthems echoing to the sky.

And the trees clap their hands, and winds rejoice
   In the deep chorus which themselves prolong,
Worshipping God with grand and glorious voice,
   And sending heavenward their triumphant song.

In spring and summer the calm zephyrs sigh,
   In whispering melody and gentle love,
As though some soft æolian harp were nigh,
   Breathing heart-worship to the throne above.

And the birds sing in courses all the year;
   'Midst leafless boughs the ever-buoyant thrush
Pours his melodious hymn till spring is here,
   And loftier notes of living rapture gush,

When nightingales are leaders of the choir,   ·
   And praise incessant fills and charms the ear,
And solemn watch-night harmonies inspire,
   And matin-anthems rise when day draws near.

And oft when autumn sinks in winter's gloom,
   The robin redbreast from his lonely perch
Sings his low requiem o'er nature's tomb,
   The sole precentor of the woodland church.

Nature is full of God, creation yields
   Perpetual homage in unconscious praise;
And birds, and beasts, and winds, and flowery fields,
   Vocal or silent, still their offerings raise.

With bended knees and lifted hands we bow
   Beneath this vernal roof of oak and birch,
And worship God, and here renew our vow
   Before the altar of the woodland church.

SABBATH MORNING.

THE Sabbath dawns, and with its first appear-
　　ing
　　Comes a soft hush of quiet o'er the earth,
And on the gentle breeze love whispers,
　　cheering
　　Our hearts to holy mirth.

Blest Sabbath! how can language tell thy sweetness?
　　Firstborn of Eden, evermore divine,
Earth's weekly sacrament and heaven's completeness
　　Ineffable, are thine.

Stream in the arid desert, ever flowing,
　　River of life, whose fountain is on high,
Waters to swim in, wheresoever going,
　　Thou carriest health and joy.

Earth's jubilee, still week by week returning,
　　With trumpet-blast proclaiming Heaven's decree,—
That men may satisfy their souls' deep yearning,
　　And be from sin set free.

O scented flower! amid earth's sandy waste
　　Blooming, a gem of paradise and love ;
Unsullied by the fall, and all as chaste
　　As heaven's pure flowers above.

White dove celestial! 'midst the tempest dark,
    And sorrow's hurricane, and sin's increase,
Speeding on Sundays to our lonely ark
       With olive branch of peace.

Hope to the hopeless comes, and joy in sorrow,
    And healing balm to hearts by anguish pained,
And life in death; for Sabbaths bring the morrow
       Of life eternal gained.

Heaven's vestibule, we breathe the breath immortal,
    While yet through the world's wilderness we roam,
And stand all glorious in the glittering portal
       Of our eternal home.

And week by week, in beautiful transition,
    From grace to grace we rise with heaven to blend,
And every Sabbath day brings a new vision
       Of Sabbaths without end.

SABBATH WORSHIP.

DAY of days! with heaven's own radiance
    shining,
  Blest Sabbath! welcome is thy hallowed
    rest ;
Thy influence, elevating and refining,
    Gives life its purest zest.

Thou comest weekly with the balm of healing,
  Like good Samaritan, in love divine ;
Over our wounds of sin and sorrow kneeling,
    To pour in oil and wine.

The bliss of Eden is again perennial,
  And peace and purity resume their sway ;
And in His garden, bright with flowers millennial,
    God walks on this sweet day.

Prelude of heaven in sanctified affection,
  And loving unison which never dies,
To-day we antedate the resurrection—
    The dead in sin arise.

Amidst the candlesticks, all bright and golden,
  To-day Christ walks in royalty and might,
The broken-hearted sinner to embolden,
    And turn his gloom to light.

On Sunday shines the ever-fiery column
    Which shields the pilgrim Church from all her foes ;
In splendour yet more terrible and solemn
      The flaming pillar glows.

So on the Sabbath, from heaven's glittering portal
    Came down the tongues of fire and rushing wind,
The glorious mystery of life immortal
      Revealed to all mankind.

And so again, wrought out of earth's confusion,
    And jarring elements, o'erruled for good,
And the almighty power of truth's diffusion,
      This world shall be renewed.

And then the Sabbath will be universal,
    And Christ shall reign in triumph all His own ;
And all our Sabbath songs be a rehearsal
      For worship round the throne ;

Where the Church militant in countless millions
    Shall join the Sabbath of the Church above,
And walk the golden floor of heaven's pavilions,
      For ever lost in love.

SABBATH REST.

THE Sabbath is a type of heaven's own
    sweetness,
    A hallowed foretaste of its life and light ;
A day of rest, foreshadowing the completeness
    Of days which have no night.

Six days of weariness and toil, succeeded
    By the calm quietude of Sabbath rest,
Train us to welcome what we so much needed,
    And make it doubly blest.

Here our best joys and fairest flowers are mortal—
    We only rest in peace one day in seven ;
But yonder, soon as we pass death's dread portal,
    Eternal rest is given.

The Sabbath here, in high communion blending
    With Christ, and all the heaven-bound pilgrim train,
Is more than blessed, but soon has its ending,
    And earth is earth again.

But yonder, in the land of milk and honey,
    Where Jordan flows, rest is for evermore ;
One everlasting Sabbath, bright and sunny,
    Shines on that blissful shore.

All is immortal there ! joys never wither,
   And days no longer shadow into night ;
With steady pace our feet are travelling thither,
     To gain that land of light.

O happy Sabbath ! when the Church shall gather,
   Escaped for ever from time's wearying strife,
Like children round the table of their Father,
     To live the deathless life,

And swell the rapturous song of adoration
   With all who fought the fadeless crown to win.
O endless Sabbath ! chorus of salvation !
     When will thy joys begin ?

ETERNITY.

ETERNITY! eternity!
　　How near thou art to me!
　　When shall thine endless day begin,
　　　And time no longer be?
When shall earth's veil be rent
　　In twain, and no more sea,
And life in one word blent,—
　　Eternity! eternity!

Eternity! eternity!
　　What art thou? answer now.
The youth of endless ages,
　　No wrinkle on thy brow;
A day which had no dawning,
　　And never night shall see,
An everlasting morning—
　　Eternity! eternity!

The life that soareth ever
　　Upwards, and spurns decay;
Maturity maturing
　　In growth that knows no stay.
Depths below line or plummet,
　　Fathomless! dazzling heights
Which have nor path nor summit,
　　Beyond archangels' flights!

God's lifetime—the foundation
   Whereon His throne was raised
Ages before creation,
   Ere man or angel praised ;
Before sun, moon, or stars
   Outflashed their primal light,
Or heaven had rebel wars,
   Or day was born, or night.

The charter of heaven's glory,
   The sum of angels' joys,
Age never growing hoary,
   And bliss which never cloys.
The full reward awaiting,
   When death no more shall sever ;
Eternal bliss, creating
   Eternal bliss for ever !

Eternity ! eternity !
   The dwelling-place of God ;
The jasper walls and golden streets
   Are there, by angels trod.
The river of salvation
   And tree of life are there ;
And saints in constellation,
   Christ's stars, shine bright and fair.

Heaven's glittering pavilions,
   Those mansions of the blest,
Filled with triumphant millions,
   There in the promised rest.

No more by sorrow smitten,
  From sin and death set free,
On every joy is written,
  Eternity! eternity!

Eternity! eternity!
  O haven of joy unpriced!
O rapture beyond utterance!
  Eternity with Christ!
'Midst holy angels bending,
  With glorious martyrs joined
In chants and songs unending,
  Ineffable, refined.

Eternity! eternity!
  With bodies like our Lord,
Glowing with immortality,
  In holiness restored;
Heaven's crystal heights exploring,
  Mysterious and unknown,
Or silently adoring
  The Lamb upon the throne.

Eternity! eternity!
  I feel thee near to me;
So very near, I seem to hear
  Heaven's holy minstrelsy.
Hush! there's a voice on the night's calm
  Comes, as I bend my knee,
Solemn and sweet as angel's psalm,
  "Eternity! eternity!"

ANGEL VISITS.

HAVE you heard an angel's whisper,
   Or the cadence of a hymn
Sung by a voice celestial,
   Some radiant cherubim ?
Once in the lonely woodland,
   Beneath the harvest moon,
Entranced, I knelt and listened,
   At midnight's solemn noon.

The earth lay round me sleeping
   In undisturbed repose,
And zephyrs stayed their breathing,
   And not a sound arose ;
The nightingale's sweet trillings
   Of melody had gushed
Upon my ravished ear, but now
   Her warbling voice was hushed.

It was the reign of silence,
   The aspen leaves were still
And motionless as death,
   While stars, at their sweet will,

Looked down in radiance loving ;
  So did the full round moon,
While all my thoughts rose heavenwards
  At that calm midnight noon.

A gentle voice spoke softly
  In words of peace and love,
Of higher, nobler being
  Awaiting us above ;
Of dear ones with the angels
  Who once were here below,
Waiting till we rejoin them,
  And their high glory know.

Of heaven, where knowledge knoweth,
  And the mind's comprehension
Expands for ever, grasping
  Unlimited extension ;
Where God, and life eternal,
  And purity, and joy,
Fill the immortal spirit
  With bliss without alloy.

Then came such strains of melody
  Ethereal on my ears,
As evermore is echoing
  Along those happier spheres.
Surely the song of angels
  That summer night I heard,
And my inmost soul adoring
  With those high hymns was stirred.

Was it a dream ?   So holy
    That night was every thought,
That woodland was a sacred place,
    With heavenly blessing fraught.
And still those angel whispers,
    And the cadence of those songs
Heard on that summer midnight,
    My memory prolongs.

THE WINTER VIOLET.

THE purple violet, blooming and sweet-scented,
  Breathes its rich perfume on the wintry air
On a south bank, beneath green leafage tented,
    In hidden beauty rare.

Where withered leaves fell rustling all around it,
  Cradled in snow, and dandled in the storm,
Smiling in summer loveliness, I found it
    In its most perfect form.

So the pure fragrance of a life devoted
  To virtue's loving deeds, and others' good,
Is wafted, like the violet scent, and noted,
    With living power endued.

And this lone violet a lesson teaches
  Of modest meekness, screened from public view,
Blessing the sight and scent where'er it reaches,
    In bloom the winter through.

Beautiful violet! all in flower so cheery,
  Breathe out the incense of thy welcome scent;
To loving hearts e'en winter is not dreary
    In acts of kindness spent.

TO A DAISY ON CHRISTMAS DAY.

THOUGH the day is dark and dreary,
　　On a sunward slope I see
One sweet, modest little daisy,
　　And it seems to look at me.
Opened in its simple beauty,
　　Waiting for the sunshine ray,
Feeling it a daisy's duty
　　To look glad on Christmas day.

All around the snow is lying,
　　But on one small plot of green,
Where the southern breeze came sighing,
　　My own daisy sprung between;
Fully blown as in the summer,
　　Lovely in its pale array;
Welcome, innocent new comer,
　　On this happy Christmas day.

May I take thee, guest unbidden,
　　To the feast of Him new-born,
And with scents of heart-myrrh hidden,
　　Offer thee, this joyous morn?
Thou wild daisy, blooming sweetly,
　　Like the star of Bethlehem's ray
Shinest, in thy whiteness meetly
　　Smiling on this Christmas day.

FOR CHRISTMAS DAY.

RING out, merry bells, over mountains and fells,
    At the dawning of morn,
And spread the glad news that Jesus is born;
From their glorious abode, bright angels of
    God
    Come down to the earth,
And in carols of joy they publish His birth.

And Bethlehem's star, which shines from afar,
    Stands over the place
Where the Infant lies wrapped in His mother's embrace;
And the star's golden flame, like an orient gem
    Set in royalty's crown,
Shows the Infant divine, and God is made known.

He comes to reverse the original curse,
    And ransom our race;
Encircling the world in the arms of His grace.
In infinite love He descends from above,
    Redeemer and Lord,
A new Eden to bring, by His coming restored.

So the curse is repealed, and the flowers of the field
    And the trees of the wood
Smile in verdure, and beauty, and blessing renewed.

D

And the bountiful earth heaves with joy at His birth,
  And ocean's wild form
Pays homage to Him who rides on the storm.

Ring out, merry bells, in musical swells,
  And round the glad hearth
Let the theme of our songs be Jesus's birth.
Ring out, merry bells, and where happiness dwells
  And loving ones meet,
The loudest hosannas our Saviour shall greet.

THE STAR OF BETHLEHEM.

THE Star of Bethlehem, with light increasing,
Still pours its heavenly radiance on the
earth ;
God's lamp, which marks with lustre never
ceasing,
The place of Jesu's birth,

And spreads the news o'er continent and sea,
Through the four quarters of the ransomed world,
That all the Star of Bethlehem may see,
In widening beams unfurled.

That pilgrims in the track of Eastern sages
May flow by millions to the humble shrine,
And swell the mighty song of coming ages,
The angels' song divine.

On the broad ocean—in the desert dreary—
In crowded cities—o'er the forest wide—
Where the sick lie in pain and suffering weary—
From morn to eventide.

In gloomy Greenland—at the Arctic pole,
Where the poor Esquimaux contented toils,
Wherever man is found, and seasons roll,
The Star of Bethlehem smiles.

And angel harmonies still softly sound
    Over our heads, and all our senses thrill
With songs immortal—joy and love abound,
      Sweet peace and heaven's good-will.

Our Christmas songs are angels' songs repeated,
    And festive gatherings may not happy be,
Unless the Guest divine be with us seated,
      The Guest of Bethany.

Sweet Babe of Bethlehem ! on whose lowly manger
    The glittering diamond blazes in the sky,
Star-crowned, we worship Thee, thou royal Stranger,
      And join the choir on high.

Like Thee, blest Babe ! in humble guise and lowly
    Would we, all careless of earth's smile or frown,
Bear, with submission ever meek and lowly,
      The cross, and win the crown.

HYMN TO CHRIST.

JESUS our King!
    We worship Thee now,
Exultingly sing
    While lowly we bow.
Like Stephen we cry,
    Beholding Thee stand
All glorious on high,
    At Thy Father's right hand.

Our Advocate Thou,
    Our Priest evermore,
Whose prevalent prayer
    Pleads the sorrow He bore;
To the Lamb that was slain
    Our voices we raise,
Hallelujah again
    We shout to His praise.

O Jesus our King!
    We think of Thy woes,
Thy sufferings to bring
    Us joy and repose.
The cross Thou hast borne
    Amidst agony deep,
All bleeding and torn,—
    And singing, we weep.

O Jesus our King!
    We tell of Thy might,
Thy victories sing,
    Thy conquests in fight.
Temptation, and sin,
    And Satan o'erthrown,
Our pardon to win,
    And Thy love to make known.

Ride on in Thy might,
    O Saviour divine;
Establish Thy right,
    Earth's millions are Thine.
In Thy kingdom restored,
    Inherit Thine own,
Omnipotent Lord,
    O set up Thy throne.

Earth! sound forth the power
    Of Jesus our King,
The Ancient of days
    Triumphantly sing;
All glory is due,
    All worship be given,
In songs ever new,
    On earth and in heaven.

COVENANT HYMN.

FOR THE CLOSET.

BLESSED Jesus! at Thy word
 I shut my closet door,
Kneeling down to seek my Lord,
 Obedient evermore.
Silent, prostrate, and alone,
 Bowing lowly at Thy feet,
Make Thy saving mercy known,
 Thy waiting servant meet.

Through Thy sacrificial blood,
 And all-availing prayer,
Now bestow the peace of God,
 And Thy new name declare.
Naked is my heart to Thee,
 Claim it as Thy rightful due;
Let me now, from sin set free,
 My covenant renew.

"My Beloved" now "is mine,"
 And tells me "I am His;"
Sanctified by love divine,
 I taste immortal bliss.

Joined to Christ, my living Head,
   I feel the deathless life begun ;
Banquet on celestial bread,
   And I and Christ are one.

One for ever ! life or death
   Shall never part us more,
Quickened by the Spirit's breath,
   The death of sin is o'er.
Jesus and His boundless grace,
   All the virtue of His blood,
All are mine, and through His face
   I see the face of God.

Jesus ! own my covenant vow,
   And bid my faith increase ;
Breathe on me, and give me now
   Thy legacy of peace.
Purge me with refining fire,
   Be the hallowing meekness given ;
Till I join the upper choir,
   And shout Thy praise in heaven.

COVENANT HYMN.

FOR THE SANCTUARY.

ASSEMBLED we join,
    In Jesus's name,
In rapture divine
    His praise to proclaim;
Our voices unite
    With angels above,
Who day without night
    Rejoice in His love.

The ransomed of God,
    With glad hearts and tongues,
Through covenant blood
    Returning with songs;
Our heads we lift up,
    And triumphantly cry,
"Our glorious hope
    Of redemption is nigh!"

Redemption from sin
    Through Christ is made known,
The kingdom within
    Through Him is our own;

And strong in the Lord,
   And the power of His might,
We trust in His word
   And walk in His light.

As the heart of one man
   We covenant make,
Nor Satan nor hell
   Can our covenant shake ;
" Abba, Father," we cry
   By the Spirit divine,
On earth and on high
   Eternally Thine !

Eternally Thine,
   Till with palm and with crown
We drink the new wine,
   And with Jesus sit down
'Midst the glorified throng
   In the ranks of the blest,
And swell the new song
   With the weary at rest.

Ineffably one
   With all His elect,
Our Lord on His throne
   We meekly expect ;
And fellowship hold
   In His earthly abode,
With the Catholic fold
   And the Covenant God.

FOR PALM SUNDAY.

ONE day of gladness—but without a morrow—
    Smiled on our Saviour's thorny path below;
Shining with brightness through a cloud of
        sorrow,
    Darkening to deeper woe.

From Bethany and Bethphage, onward going
    Towards Jerusalem, to suffer there,
The quenchless fire of love divine still glowing,
    For us the cross to bear.

Hark! how the slopes of Olivet are ringing
    With loud hosannas to the peaceful King!
While the whole multitude break forth in singing,
    And festal offerings bring.

Still upward winding to the mountain's brow,
    Behold the wonderful procession pass;
And to the lowly King of Zion bow,
    Riding upon an ass.

See how they spread their garments out before Him,
    And strew His sacred path with branching palm;
But while they spread His triumphs, and adore Him,
    He rides in silence calm.

For soon—just as the showers of April burst
   When a black cloud athwart the sky appears—
The glowing hallelujah is reversed,
     And songs are changed to tears.

The mountain summit opened to His view
   Jerusalem, where martyred prophets slept ;
And when He saw the city, He foreknew
     Her coming woes, and wept.

So whilst the crowd, all jubilant descending
   The steeps of Olivet, His praise prolong,
The blessed Jesus weeps, His tears are blending
     With their triumphant song.

I.—FOR GOOD FRIDAY.

CHRIST our passover is slain,
    For us the Victim bleeds,
On the Cross He bears our pain,
    And there for sinners pleads.
Crushed beneath the dreadful load,
    Hear His groans! His sufferings see!
"Why," He cries, "My God! My God!
Hast Thou forsaken Me?"

Earth and hell in league unite,
    And men with devils join;
Him, the Son of God, to smite
    And trample, they combine.
Scourged, and crowned with thorns, and nailed
    His loving arms extended wide,
There in agony impaled,
    The Man of sorrows died.

Earthquakes rend the solid ground,
    The shrouded dead arise,
Rocks are riven, and all around
    Behold the darkened skies.

Severed is the temple's veil,
   While nature, in convulsive throes,
Moans in sympathetic wail,
   Unutterable woes.

O Thou dying Lamb of God !
   Around Thy Cross we bow ;
Bending down beneath our load
   Of sin, we worship now.
Guilty, wretched, and undone,
   Thou hast died that we might live,
Ransomed by Thy blood alone,
   To Thee our hearts we give.

II.—FOR GOOD FRIDAY.

HANGING upon the Cross, with arms extended,
    And hands nail-pierced, and fastened to
        the wood,
    With all intensities of suffering blended,
    And bathed in His own blood.
See ! sinner, see ! the meek and loving Jesus
    Writhing in agony, all pale and wan,
Bearing our guilt, He suffers to release us,
    Sinners ! behold the man !

His head, thorn-crowned and bloody, droops in anguish ;
    His feet—hark how they nail them to the tree !
Hung there six dreadful hours, to groan and languish,
        Sinner ! for thee ! for thee !
Hear how He moans, by earth and heaven forsaken ;
    Hear His lone agony of suffering burst,
While echoing mountains are by earthquake shaken
        At Jesus' cry, "I thirst ! "

The sun goes out in night,—and the hills, reeling,
    Heave to their base in sympathetic dread ;
Earth trembles, and amidst loud thunders pealing,
    The graves give up their dead.

'Mid torrents of revilings undiminished,
    And bitter gibes and scoffings, fierce and loud,
With one last awful utterance, " It is finished ! "
      His head in death is bowed.

But vengeance still outlives His calm submission,
    A soldier thrusts his spear in Jesus' side,
And blood and water from that deep incision
      Flow in a mingled tide.
O Lamb of God ! with my heart's love embracing,
    I clasp Thy Cross, and kiss Thy wounded feet,
Weeping for joy, and in my soul's abasing,
      My grief and bliss complete.

EASTER EVE.

 THOU sweet Saviour! at Thy grave I wait,
Kneeling in sorrow, for my grief is great,
But worshipping my Lord in low estate.

The Roman soldiers, pacing to and fro,
Guard Thy sealed sepulchre from friend and foe,
But nothing of Thy power or love they know.

I wept all yesterday to see Thee slain,
And now my tears for Thee flow down again,
To think that Thou shouldst suffer such deep pain.

Scorned, mocked, and smitten, earth and hell allied
To nail Thee to the cross and pierce Thy side,
And crush Thee in Thy meekness deified.

The storm which beat upon Thy blessed head
Still echoes in my heart, and still I dread,
And shudder still, to see Thee dying, dead!

Dead on the cross! suspended in Thy blood!
And now in this cold grave is Thy abode,
O Lord and Saviour, O meek Lamb of God!

E

How still this garden is !   The olives wave,
Swayed by the midnight breeze, over Thy grave,—
Thy grave, who lived to love and died to save.

Let me behold Thee when the glittering stars
Melt into morning, when Thy prison bars
Are burst, and Thou com'st forth in scars

All glorious ! marks of victory and death,
Of man redeemed, drawing immortal breath,
And all God's family of one pure faith.

Let me behold Thee, and embrace Thy feet,
And weep awhile in joy and sorrow meet,
And on my knees Thy resurrection greet.

Let me behold Thee, O my conquering Lord,
On Thine ascension day ; Thy parting word
Of peace be mine,—'twere paradise restored.

Let me behold Thee when, on clouds descending,
Thou com'st to judgment—when the heavens are rending,
And saints and angels are in pomp attending.

Then, 'midst a flaming world, with terror rife,
And falling suns and stars in fiery strife,
Give me, my glorious Lord, a crown of life.

LOVE TO CHRIST.

JESUS! Thy precious name is sweet;
In love I weep and kiss Thy feet,—
Thy sacred feet transfixed for me,
And nailed in anguish to the tree.

'Midst Gentile hate, and Jewish scorn,
With arms outstretched, and crowned with
  thorn,
Six weary hours upon the tree,
To save the chief of sinners, me.

O Jesus! name most dear and sweet,
My risen Lord I haste to greet;
In love intense of heart and soul,
And rapturous joy beyond control.

My life, my crown, my hope and rest,
My all I have, of Thee possest;
If Jesus' smile to me be given,
I ask not for a higher heaven.

O sacred scars! O wounded side!
For me my Lord was crucified:
But the dread pains of that lone strife
With death and hell, bring peace and life.

Let me but Jesus love and know,
Then storms may howl and tempests blow ;
My happiness will yet increase,
Nor earth nor hell shall break my peace.

O Jesus ! let me ever prove
Thine in deep tenderness of love ;
And lowly leaning on Thy breast,
Find there my soul's eternal rest.

THE FAITHFUL SOLDIER.

FAITHFUL soldier! are thy conflicts ended?
    Armour of God, and sword, and shield,
        laid down?
Thy battle-shouts with victory's songs were
        blended,
    And on the cross, thy crown.

O valiant warrior! in thy long campaigning
    Thy mighty sword was never sheathed or blunt;
But thou wert evermore fresh conquests gaining,
    And in the battle's front.

Fighting for thy dear Lord, His standard waving;
    Courageous ever, ever in the field;
Faithful to death wast thou, all danger braving,
    And rather die than yield.

Conquering and on to conquer, stern, untiring,
    Battling for Christ, His heritage to claim;
Thy fellow-soldiers with new zeal inspiring,
    And love for Jesus' name.

Now thou art resting on the field of glory,
    Buried by comrades with their arms reversed,
And by the camp-fires often is the story
    Of thy brave deeds rehearsed.

AT A DEATH-BED.

ITHIN a quiet chamber, hushed, apart,
    There lay a dying saint,
    Made perfect now through suffering,
        pure in heart,
And bearing without murmur or complaint
    Her heavenly Father's rod—
    Made meet to see her God.

Opening her chamber window, the soft breeze,
    With summer's odours laden, came in sighing,
As if in sympathy, to soothe, and ease,
    And cool her fevered brow as she lay dying.
When a low whisper rose upon the ear,—
    "How gracious is my God, my Father,
        To send these gentle zephyrs from above!
They feel like heaven's own breathing,
Or chaplets round my forehead wreathing;
    I would not longer linger, I had rather
    Go to my heavenly Father—
        God is love! God is love!"

A friendly hand brought flowers,
    Fresh-gathered flowers, into that dying room;
And as the meadows after showers
    Are sweet for hours,

Such was their rich perfume
'Midst the pure sanctity of that sick room.
" God loves me still ! " in accents low she spoke,
   " Do I smell spices from the land of rest ?
A box of alabaster has been broke—
   My soul is doubly blest :
The gain and bliss of dying now I prove—
   God is love ! God is love ! "

A sunbeam, struggling through the leafy shade,
   Between the roses round the window twining,
Fell on her bed and glittered there.
Her thin pale hands, enclasped in prayer,
   Were on her bosom laid ;
   Her pallid face, with radiance shining,
   Her inward peace displayed.
   And then, in faltering words, she said,
" O joy unspeakable ! O bliss unknown !
   This sunshine, smiling from above,
Is God's—God's sunshine from His throne,
   And it comes streaming down,
   My death to crown—
God is love ! God is love ! "

A gentle footfall sounded on the stair,
   And, by her bedside kneeling,
The loving pastor bent in prayer,
   In the deep tones of feeling.
And then she took the sacred bread
   Of life divine ;
And then the blood for sinners shed,
   The eucharistic wine.

O hallowed hour !
O mystic power !
Her raptured soul
Was filled with God, Christ's touch had made her whole.
  "Now would I die !" she cried ;
" Why do His chariot wheels so slowly move ?
    My fetters break ;
    Soon I shall wake,
  To be for ever satisfied !
God is love ! God is love ! "

That silent chamber now was holy ground,
The porch of heaven, where waiting saints are found ;
Hushed into silence every tongue,
    And God was very nigh.
It seemed too hallowed now for prayer or song,—
    Too near eternity.
Death came with softened mien,
  Shorn of his terrors and his sting ;
A moment's conflict, then the calm serene
  Of victory on wing.
" Angels are here ! I see them waiting now,"
She whispered, in a tone of solemn joy ;
    " Angels are come !
Their wings are rustling in the room—
    I long to fly.
If this be dying, oh, 'tis heaven to die !
    Jesus is mine !
  I go, like Noah's dove,
    Into the Ark divine."
Just as her spirit fled,
New beams of glory on her face were shed,—

A halo from above;
And one melodious whisper heard,
Her latest word,
    "God is love! God is love!"

CHRIST IS ALL AND IN ALL.

OST dear and precious Saviour,
   My all in all Thou art!
My constant joy, my tongue's employ,
   The life-throb of my heart.
To Thee by faith united,
   I live the life divine,
And daily prove that Jesus' love
   Unspeakable is mine.

On Jesus' breast reclining,
   His blessed words I hear,
And like a child, all meek and mild,
   Attend with listening ear.
I seek His gentle spirit,
   And, moulded to His will,
Go forth in might of love and light,
   For Jesus working still.

Most dear and precious Saviour!
   Thy blood is all my plea;
By sin enticed, I fly to Christ,
   And gain the victory.
To Christ for ever cleaving,
   In love and faith divine,
Redeemed, restored, my God and Lord,
   And all in Him is mine.

GOING TO EMMAUS.

WALKING in sad companionship of woe,
Towards Emmaus two disciples go,
Talking, with troubled hearts, in accents
low.

Perchance they wept—their loving Master gone;
They saw Him dying, and they heard Him groan,—
The Shepherd smitten, and the sheep alone!

A stranger joined them, in their grief and fear,
And soon pure words of kindness met their ear
And soothed their hearts. "Jesus himself drew near."

Spell-bound, they listened as the Stranger taught,
His knowledge deep, and clothed his every thought
In words with supernatural wisdom fraught.

Who was the Stranger, with such wisdom golden,
By whom all scriptural mysteries were unfolden?
As yet they knew not, for "their eyes were holden."

But they constrained the Stranger to abide;
So He sat down to meat, and side by side
Taught them more of Himself, till eventide.

And as He blessed the hallowed bread, and brake,
Their eyes were opened, it was Christ who spake !
And their hearts burned within them for His sake.

They saw again, and knew their risen Lord,
Jesus the Conqueror, from the grave restored,
And heard His voice around their humble board.

But while He spake, He vanished from their sight,
And left them tremulous in calm delight
Of mingled joy and wonder at the sight.

Then, journeying in haste, they swiftly sped
Back to Jerusalem, the news to spread
That Christ their Lord was risen from the dead.

FOR ASCENSION DAY.

SWEET, sacred Bethany! there dwelt the lowly
    Martha and Mary; beautiful retreat,
Where Jesus "lodged," and held communion
        holy,
    And oft sat down to meat.

Sweet, sacred Bethany! where Lazarus sickened,
    And dying, in the silent tomb he slept,
Till back to life again by Jesus quickened,
    Who at his grave-side wept.

Thy very dust, O Bethany, is dear
    To us, heart-hallowed, and we kiss thy sod
Upon our bended knees. Our souls revere
    The paths by Jesus trod.

Sweet, sacred Bethany! embalmed for ever
    In precious memories which cannot die,
Jesus and Bethany, no time can sever
    That love-cemented tie.

O glowing love! O matchless condescension!
    The sorrowing disciples by their Lord
Are led to Bethany, at His ascension,
    To hear His parting word.

His parting word falls sweetly on their ears,
    Like a soft cadence ere the music cease;
He breathes upon them, 'midst their silent tears,
      His legacy of "peace."

And, glorious promise! still to cheer their hearts
    And lift their spirits to their heavenly home,—
O blessed promise! though their Lord departs,
      The "Comforter" shall come.

So while He blessed them, slowly He arose
    Heavenward, ascending to the realms of light,
By circling clouds enshrouded as He goes,
      Soon hidden from their sight.

Earth had no hymn, and not a strain was heard,
    When the triumphant Conqueror returned,
But heaven through all its glowing ranks was stirred,
      And every bosom burned.

Uplifted were the everlasting doors,
    And every pearly gate wide open flung,
To hail the King of glory heaven adores,
      In praises here unsung.

All rapt and wondering—kneeling, and still gazing
    Heavenwards, the wondering disciples stayed,
Entranced, and filled with fears and thoughts amazing
      Of their ascended Head.

But swiftly to Jerusalem returning,
In prayer they waited all with one accord,
And knit together in one holy yearning
Of love to their dear Lord.

In waiting waited they, for ten days pleading
With deep intensity and strong desire,
Till came the answer to their interceding
In cloven tongues of fire.

SUDDEN GLORY.

(ON THE SUDDEN DEATH OF AN EMINENT MINISTER.)

S O came the summons on a Sabbath morning,
  Just as the chiming bells
Gave utterance to their ever-welcome warning,
  In modulated swells.

They chimed, in tones of soft persuasive sweetness,
  "Come to the house of prayer;"
And wooed to think of heaven, and pray for meetness
  To join the pure ones there:

When God's swift messenger, unseen but glorious,
  Came suddenly to bring
Release from earth, and waft the soul victorious
  To heaven beneath his wing.

No longer in His lower courts to render
  Worship and service here,
God called His servant to the dazzling splendour
  Of heaven, to worship there,

Amongst the angels, all in royal brightness,
  Within that high abode,
With saints and martyrs in their spotless whiteness,
  Circling the throne of God.

Rising at once to his celestial dwelling,
    On that calm Sabbath day,
For the first time to hear heaven's anthems swelling,
    And join the ceaseless lay.

So ends a life of labour unremitting,
    For love of Christ his Lord ;
With a translation every way befitting
    His work and his reward.

So lives his chaste and eloquent example
    Of zeal and love combined,
That men may imitate so rare a sample
    Of gentleness refined ;

And working bravely for their Lord and Master,
    Never by sloth enticed,
Like him may rise to bliss made grander, vaster,
    By toil, and love to Christ.

HYMN FOR WHITSUNTIDE.

AS the sunshine on the flowers
    And buds in opening spring,
  Sheds its vitalizing powers,
    New forms of life to bring;
In the winter of my heart
  So may the quick'ning Spirit divine
Living plenitude impart,
  And now arise and shine.

As the fertilizing dews
  On thirsty pastures seen,
And the gentle rain, renews
  And makes the herbage green;
So upon Thy Church around
  Let the dews of grace descend,
Heavenly influence abound,
  And showers of blessings send.

As the floods upon dry ground,
  When rivers overflow,
And refreshing streams abound,
  And fruitful harvests grow;
Parched with long-continued drought,
  Hear, O Lord, Thy Church's cry;
Be the floods of grace poured out,
  The Spirit from on high.

As of old, in tongues of flame,
  And living fire displayed,
The baptizing Spirit came,
  And shone on every head ;
Now thine ancient word fulfil,
  Be Thy Spirit's power unfurled,
Work according to Thy will,
  And save the ransomed world.

Father, by Thy boundless love,
  We ask in Jesu's name,
Send the Spirit from above,
  Set up Immanuel's reign.
Jesus, by Thy precious death
  And intercession, still we pray,
Quicken by Thy Spirit's breath,
  Thy royal power display.

All creation groans for Thee,
  In mingled war and strife,
Waiting still Thy power to see,
  Giver and Lord of life.
Come in Pentecostal might,
  And make the Church Thy blest abode ;
Darkness then shall melt in light,
  And earth be filled with God.

UNDERTONES.

HE that hath ears to hear
    May drink in exquisite sounds of peace and
        love,
    Breathed from a higher sphere
By voices soft and clear,
And feel heaven's bliss brought near,
In raptures God's elect alone may prove.

Men hear and tremble when the earthquake heaves
    The mountain from its base,
And whirlwinds scatter harvest sheaves,
    And thunders rock the place.
They hear the spring's sweet singing,
    And the songs of plenty born,
    And the rustling of the ripening corn,
Abundance bringing,
And the south wind and early rain
    Make men rejoice ;
But few ears open to the strain
    Of Nature's still small voice,—
God's whispers—loving undertones
    To loving hearts, most pure,
Heard only when the spirit owns
    And feels in calm assurance sure.

Then come into the soul,
Flowing and rising with our joy's increase,
Just as the noiseless tide's incomings roll,
  Christ's life, and God's own peace.

So, when the darkened clouds
  Of Providence frown o'er us,
And God awhile enshrouds
  Himself in wrath before us,
We hear His voice and feel His rod,
And cry, " Withdraw Thy hand, O God ! "
And struggle in a spirit unmeet,
And do not lie submissive at His feet.
  But if we learn the lesson He intends,
And our hearts' adamant melt,
  And stubborn self-will bends,
Then do we know that every stroke was dealt
  For His own loving ends.
And storm-clouds break in sunlight,
  And sterner voices cease ;
And as the sky grows bright,
  We hear His words of peace ;
The still small voice is breathing
  Soft undertones of love,
And flowers of promise, wreathing
  Around the rod, we prove.
And we joy to hear, in accents clear,
  Only heard by souls subdued
And moulding for a brighter sphere,
" Love Me ! and all things here
  Shall work eternal good ! "

When the law thunders from the flaming mount,
While we lie prostrate in the vale below,
  And memory, bewildered, fails to count
Our sins, and words to tell our woe;
  And Satan tempts with worldly pelf,
And we look round the glorious earth to see,
  While he says, " All this for thyself,
If thou wilt but fall down and worship me."
  And our allegiance wavers, and our hope
Seems crushed, and conscience, in despair,
  Has no more strength to cope
With broken law, or further dare
To do, or weep, or bear,—
  Then comes, for the soul's aiding,
The still small voice,
  Which utters no upbraiding,
But says, " Believe, look up, rejoice!"
  Most precious, yet most free,
Those sacred undertones,
Which oft, on bended knee,
  I hear and own;
Whispers divine, to me
  In love made known.
The still small voice, to sanctify and cheer
The soul which thirsts for God, with listening heart and
    ear.

THE BIBLE, THE WORD OF GOD.

BLEST be the book of God's own inspiration,
　　Whose every leaf the stamp divine may boast,
Written of old, by men of varied nation,
　　Moved by the Holy Ghost.

A sacred unction breathes from all its pages,
　　And life immortal kindles in its light ;
And the one solemn voice of bygone ages
　　Proclaims its strength and might.

Prophets, and seers, and martyrs, all uniting
　　In faith unshaken, glory in the Word ;
Clad in God's armour, and the good fight fighting,
　　. They grasped the Spirit's sword.

Millions have triumphed, passing death's cold river,
　　With conquering shouts, triumphant o'er the foe ;
And every arrow, drawn from God's own quiver,
　　Was tipped with crimson glow.

The blood-besprinkled army, ever bearing
　　On their red banner the emblazoned cross,
And the bright helmet of salvation wearing,
　　Counted all else but dross ;

And treasuring in their memory's hidden sweetness
   God's priceless words of promise and of hope,
They grew in strength and sanctified completeness,
     With earth and sin to cope.

Not learning only taught them—calm conviction,
   Wrought by the Spirit, was their certain clue
To daily peace, while God's own benediction
     Proved that His word was true.

Vain is the sceptic's bold but weak endeavour
   To shake the strong foundation of God's truth,
Which liveth and abideth, and for ever
     Glows in immortal youth.

" Speak to me only," said a dying father,
   " In words of Scripture, let my faith recline
" Not on *your* words of comfort, I had rather
     " Rest on the Word divine."

So, whosoever, in God's wide dominion,
   Rests on His word, is safe for life or death,
Till the last saint shall spread his heavenward pinion,
     And draw immortal breath.

TO A BEREAVED FRIEND.

(WRITTEN TO A MINISTER ON THE SUDDEN DEATH OF HIS WIFE.)

OD help thee, brother! human consolation
  Were vain indeed without God's promised
    aid ;
Thy loved one gone, thy hearth a desolation,
   And sunshine turned to shade.
Death's messenger came suddenly, no warning
  Told of his stealthy footstep at thy door ;
The summons-cry was heard at early morning,
   At noonday all was o'er.

The daylight broke in joy and hopeful gladness,
  And the bright prospect of deliverance smiled ;
Vain hope ! death left the widowhood of sadness
   For mother and for child.
Bride of thy youth, more dear than any other,
  Loving and loved, around thy heart entwined,
The jewel of thy home—the wife—the mother,
   To the dark grave consigned.

And yet not dark ! for on that grave of sorrow
  The rays of hope and coming glory shine,
The earnest and the surety of a morrow
   Of light and bliss divine.

Weep for the dead ! but 'mid the tempest-strife,
    Over her tomb the voice of Jesus hear,—
"I am the Resurrection and the Life !
        The endless life is near."

Let calm submission soothe thee, unaffrighted
    By grief or death ; O bow to God's decree :
Thou and thy children shall be reunited
        To her so dear to thee.
In heaven's high rapture, in refined communion,
    Where parting pangs shall never more be known,
There shall you meet her, and in deathless union
        Worship before the throne.

TIME.

TIME is flowing
  Onwards like a river,
   Always, always going,
   Rushing on for ever!
Rapids here and there,
 Niagarian falls,
Hurricanes which scare,
 Tempests wild and squalls,
  Never sleeping,
  Dashing, leaping,
  Forwards sweeping,
Foaming angry spray,
Like a torrent on its way
Let loose, which none can stay;
  Ever keeping
Seawards, night and day
  Rolling, surging,
  Onwards urging,
  Till emerging
In the broad and fathomless sea—
Ocean of eternity.

Time is flying.
 Short, shadowy, swift;
With the dead and dying,
 On, on we drift,

Smiling in joy to-day,
  But oh ! to-morrow,
Hope torn away
  Leaves only sorrow.
Minutes, hours, days, like lightning
  Suddenly flash and go,
And as our joy is brightening
  It fades in woe.
We hurry on the stream,
  Thoughtless of trouble,
And while of bliss we dream,
  We grasp a bubble.

  But time " redeeming,"
  Light comes streaming,
Light from heaven upon our way ;
  Be it short and quickly flying,
Yet, who works while it is day,
  Living, doing, dying,
Suffers nought from time's decay.
Down the rapids, o'er the falls,
Through the wild tornado-squalls,
God is with us to defend
Through the journey, to the end.

Be the passage rough and short,
Sooner shall we gain the port,
Through the surf and o'er the waves,
Heedless of the storm which raves.
    On we steer,
    Devoid of fear ;

Death is life, and time's last hour
   Brings the prize for which we strive—
The soul's immortal dower,
   And we begin to live.

THE NAME OF JESUS.

THY name, O Jesus! is the condensation
    Of heavenly beauty and celestial love ;
All harmonies divine, in concentration,
    In Thy dear name we prove.

Thy garments smell of spikenard and of myrrh,
    And cassia and aloes blend and meet
In fragrance round Thy name for evermore,
    To make our bliss complete.

Where'er Thy feet have trodden, wheresoever
    Thy loving nail-pierced hands have been outspread,
Thy agonies are still remembered ever—
    Jesus! with thorn-crowned head.

And all the gentle words Thy lips have spoken,
    Re-echoed down the centuries of time,
Live still embalmed in memories unbroken,
    Eternal and sublime.

"Husband" or "Bridegroom," "Prophet," "Priest," or
        "King,"
    Or "Mighty Counsellor," or dying "Lamb,"
All glorious titles heaven or earth can bring,
    Centre in Jesu's name.

The harps of heaven to melody are strung
   By Jesu's name, and all the ransomed choir
Shout to the name of Jesus, every tongue
   Touched with the hallowed fire.

And earth's high psalmody of loftiest praise
   Soars highest on devotion's buoyant wing
When Jesus is the subject of our lays,
   When Jesu's name we sing.

A song, with but one word of comprehension,
   A drop for brevity, and yet a sea
Of boundless depth, and infinite extension,
   In Jesu's name we see.

Two syllables,—yet, like the chorus-swelling
   Of some grand oratorio, they unite
Both heaven and earth in praise, for ever telling
   Of Jesus' power and might.

Only five letters in that wondrous name,
   The name of Jesus ; but in these combine
Earth's glorious hallelujahs to the Lamb,
   And heaven's high songs divine.

My joy, my all Thou art ! spring ever vernal
   Blooms while Thy precious name is on my tongue,
And through the cycles of the life eternal
   Jesus shall be my song.

IN MEMORIAM.

THE servant of God has laid down his load,
        And gone to his rest,
With Jesus his Lord eternally blest.
The tempest of life, with its hurricane-strife,
        Is over at last ;
In the haven of peace his anchor is cast.

The cross, meekly borne amidst conflict and scorn,
        Is exchanged for a crown ;
And the glorified saint inherits a throne.
Affliction and pain have wrought for his gain
        A glorious reward
Of ineffable joy in the light of the Lord.

Oh the rapturous songs of myriads of tongues !
        The triumph divine,
Where the rays of the Godhead transparently shine !
Oh the robes of pure white, the unsullied delight
        With Jesus to reign,
And worship for ever the Lamb that was slain !

Wouldst thou follow our friend, and to glory ascend ?
        O work for the Lord !
And publish, like him, the life-giving word.

By labour and care, and omnipotent prayer,
        Be it thine to press on,—
The battle to-day, and to-morrow the crown.

"Follow on!" hear him cry, from his home in the sky,—
        "The kingdom of heaven
Will only to valiant soldiers be given!"
"O victor! thy love we covet to prove,
        And thy mantle to wear,
And fight until death, thy triumph to share!"

THE BEAUTIFUL RIVER.

COME to this beautiful river,
   Whose waters as crystal are bright,
Flowing on—flowing for ever,
   Bespangled with lustre and light.
From the throne of God and the Lamb
This beautiful river comes down,
And *all* its pure waters may claim,
   Without money or price, as their own.
      O come to this beautiful river,
         Ye sinners, the vilest and worst;
         Only drink of this water, and never,
         Never again shall ye thirst.

Of this beautiful river to drink,
   Of fitness your *thirst* is the sum;
And Jesus is seen on its brink,
   Inviting the thirsty to come.
The lips most polluted with sin
   May drink of this fountain of love;
O drink! and thou shalt be made clean,
   And happy as angels above.

O come to this beautiful river,
   Away from the world and its strife;
Twelve manner of fruits, for ever,
   Grow on the tree of life.

The leaves of the tree are for healing,
   On the banks of this river divine;
O drink, while mercy is sealing
   Thy heart, and Jesus is thine.

This beautiful river is deep
   As the fathomless mercy of God;
And rolls in its measureless sweep
   At the threshold of every abode.
Its banks overflow, and its streams
   Carry life wherever they go;
And Nature more beautiful seems
   Where the waters most overflow.

O come to this beautiful river,
   Ye hungry, and thirsty, and poor;
O drink! for God is the Giver,
   And still He has mercy in store.
Ye thirsty, no longer delay!
   Ye hungry, come hither for food!
Cast your sins and your sorrows away,
   And plunge in this river of God.

O come to this beautiful river,
   Which ever is full to the brim;
Wouldst thou live and be happy for ever,
   O drink of this life-giving stream.
Why, sinner, from happiness roam,
   And dying of thirst, will you sink?
While Jesus invites you to come
   To the water of life, and drink.

O come to this beautiful river,
   Ye sinners, the vilest and worst;
Only drink of this water, and never,
   Never again shall ye thirst.

THERE IS MERCY IN JESUS FOR THEE.

(TUNE—" *There's a light in the window for thee.*")

HERE is mercy in Jesus for thee, brother,
There is mercy in Jesus for thee;
Whoever will come, in His arms there is room,
There is mercy in Jesus for thee.
This mercy is free as the air,
For every poor sinner and me;
And the sweet words of Gospel declare
There is mercy in Jesus for thee.

There is pardon and peace for us all, brother,
When the covenant blood is our plea;
Pray the publican's prayer, never yield to despair,
There is mercy in Jesus for thee.

There is fulness of joy for us all, brother,
As soon as to Jesus we flee;
For the stream of God's love flows down from above—
There is mercy in Jesus for thee.

The fountain is open for thee, brother,
If thou wilt from thy sins be set free;
On this happy day thou may'st wash them away,
There is mercy in Jesus for thee.

There is strength for the battle of life, brother,
  And thou shalt more than conqueror be;
In the good fight of faith, fight on until death—
  There is mercy in Jesus for thee.

There's a beautiful prospect for thee, brother,
  O'er the river of death we may see;
When the cross we lay down for a palm and a crown—
  There is mercy in Jesus for thee.

CHRIST IN THE HEART.

JESUS! my all in all Thou art,
Enthroned for ever in my heart,
　To sway Thy sceptre there.
Earth were a desert dark and drear,
Were not my Saviour ever near ;
　On Him I cast my care.

Leaning upon His sacred breast,
　I find in Him my joy and rest,
And still delight to prove
His uttermost salvation mine ;
And body, spirit, soul, resign
　To Jesus' faithful love.

United to my living Head
I live the deathless life, and fed
　With bread sent down from heaven,
I feel the sacrificial blood
Applied, and feast on angels' food,
　By Jesus daily given.

Jesus ! my all in all Thou art ;
More of Thy hallowing love impart,
　And all my sin remove.
Accomplish all Thy will in me,
Then lift me up with joy to see
　And dwell with Thee above.

RETURNING TO GOD.

COMING back to Thee, my God,
   I give my wanderings o'er ;
Make Thy Temple my abode,
   My dwelling evermore.
God, my God in Christ, I own,
   Loving Thee with calm delight ;
Worship toward Thy holy throne,
   And serve Thee day and night.

Lifting up my face to God
   With confidence I pray—
Lord ! remove Thy chastening rod,
   O turn Thy wrath away !
Fill my soul with joy and peace,
   And give me power to conquer sin ;
O bring near Thy righteousness,
   And make me pure within.

Then my heart shall be Thy shrine,
   All sanctified by love ;
Filled with God, and made divine,
   I heaven on earth shall prove.
Cleansed from every sinful stain,
   And washed in Jesu's precious blood,
I my paradise regain
   In fellowship with God.

A SACRAMENTAL HYMN.

IN remembrance of our Lord,
    Our Sacrifice and Priest,
    We, obedient to His word,
    Partake this holy feast.
One in penitential faith,
    Accept the privilege divine,
In the emblems of His death,
    The mystic bread and wine.

Thus we show to all mankind,
    Until He comes again,
Jesus, on the cross resigned,
    For us to suffer pain.
See His agony and sweat !
    O behold the crimson flood
Flowing from His hands and feet
    In streams of sacred blood !

Jesus dies that we may live,
    For all our sins atones ;
Life eternal we receive,
    The purchase of His groans.
On the cross our curse He bore,
    Wounded in the sinner's stead ;
There the crown of thorns He wore,
    And there He bowed His head.

Feed we now on angels' food,
    The bread of heaven is ours ;
Life we have through Jesus' blood,
    And feel its quickening powers ;
Sanctified and filled with love
    To Christ, and all who bear His name,
Till we rise to share above
    The supper of the Lamb.

ZION'S GLORY.

FOR thy sake, O Mount Zion,
    I will not hold my peace ;
Mingling my prayers with weeping,
    For thee and thine increase.
Jerusalem the holy,
    My refuge and my home,
When shall I see the brightness
    Of thy salvation come ?

Jerusalem the royal,
    Where dwelleth Zion's King,
Enthroned in regal splendour,
    His reign of peace to bring ;
Whose sceptre of dominion
    Is swayed o'er earth and sea :
How rich, and pure, and blessed
    Must that fair city be !

No longer termed forsaken,
    No longer desolate ;
But Hephzibah and Beulah
    Are blazoned on thy gate,
Thou crown of glory shining
    With precious stones most bright,
For God will make Mount Zion
    His city of delight.

Awake ! awake, O Zion !
   Jerusalem the free !
Adorn thee with thy jewels,
   The Bride of Christ to be.
Thy prayers shall soon be answered,
   The heavenly Bridegroom come ;
And Jesus, God's anointed,
   In Zion fix His home.

DEDICATION HYMN.

(FOR OPENING A PLACE OF WORSHIP.)

No. 1.

HALLELUJAH to God in His earthly abode!
　　With joy we unite,
And anthems of grateful thanksgiving indite;
With labour and prayer and diligent care
　　The work was begun,
For the glory of God, and the love of His Son.

Now gathering in throngs, with glad hearts and tongues,
　　We joyously meet.
The building is raised, the temple complete.
O walk round about, and triumphantly shout,
　　Mount Zion is ours!
Her beautiful walls, her bulwarks and towers.

By the good hand of God, this hallowed abode
　　Is a sanctified place;
With walls of salvation, and topstone of grace.
Now with chanting and laud, we magnify God,
　　And solemnly cry,
Lord and Giver of life, descend from on high!

Let Thy presence be here ; O Jesus, draw near
            This temple Thy shrine !
O fill it with light and glory divine.
Let the covenant blood of the crucified God,
            On Calvary shed,
To sinners, by thousands, bring life from the dead.

DEDICATION HYMN.

No. 2.

RISE, O Lord, into Thy rest,
   And make this mount of Zion blest
   With royal dainties richly stored,—
   A habitation for the Lord.

Here let Thy ark of strength abide,
Thy Church in every trouble hide;
Thy priests—made free from sin's alloy—
Be clothed with righteousness and joy.

Thy chosen seat, O God, maintain;
Upon Thy throne, O Jesus, reign;
Amidst the candlesticks of gold
Still walk, and still Thy love unfold.

Here may the penitent be fed
With pardoning grace, and heavenly bread;
And sinners, from their sins released,
Partake the sacramental feast.

Here may the horn of David bud
Victorious, through Jesu's blood,
And thousands, groaning to be free,
Cry, " God be merciful to me."

Let Jesu's foes be clothed with shame,
And earth and heaven adore His name,
Till wearing His millennial crown,
The King of glory shall come down.

DEDICATION HYMN.

No. 3.

GOD the Father! full of grace,
Dwell within this holy place;
Still, as in the days of old,
Thy great deep of love unfold;
Shining from the mercy-seat,
Here Thy waiting people meet.

God the Son! for ever be
With us when we worship Thee;
By Thine agony and sweat,
By Thy Cross uplifted yet,
Hear us, Jesus, when we cry;
Lamb of God, draw nigh, draw nigh.

God the Spirit! in Thy might,
Speak, and kindle life and light;
Quicken, save, and guide, and bless,
Fill our souls with righteousness;
When the gospel sound is heard,
Fall on those that hear the word.

Holy Trinity! give ear
To the worship offered here;
Triune God, this Temple own,
Make our hearts Thy living throne;
So shall daily incense rise
To Thy Temple in the skies.

DEDICATION HYMN.

No. 4.

FOR ever may this House of prayer
  Be hallowed by the light divine,
And standing, beautiful and fair,
  Fulfil its sanctified design,—
The home of mourners in distress,
For earthly joy and heavenly grace.

Here may the glorious gospel word
  Be preached in purity and power,
And here the Spirit's two-edged sword,
  In flaming majesty, devour
The stubble and the chaff of sin,
And new and growing triumphs win.

By Jesu's gentle words enticed,
  Most welcome, by His mercy sought,
Here may young children come to Christ,
  And, by believing parents brought,
Receive the true baptismal sign,
The quickening breath of life divine.

And kneeling at the Saviour's feet,
  Here may we feed on angels' food,
By faith the broken Body eat,
  And drink His sacrificial blood ;
One with the Church below, and one
With that triumphant round the throne.

With all who own our common Lord,
  We join in catholic embrace,
And pray for unity restored
  To all the family of grace ;
Around one Father's table fed,
And one in Christ, their living Head.

GETHSEMANE.

FROM the last supper and its closing hymn,
As the night-shadows gathered thick and dim,
Came Jesus forth, and crossing Cedron's stream,

With His eleven disciples, sad and lone,
He sought Mount Olivet—as often prone
To pray there, but to-night to weep and groan.

O the deep agony of that dread hour!
That awful night of Satan's fiercest power,
When drops of blood fell down,—a crimson shower.

Withdrawn a stone's cast from all human aid,
Alone He wrestled, and alone He prayed,
Smitten in anguish,—soon to be betrayed.

"If it be possible," with threefold groan,
"Let this cup pass," He cried, in pangs unknown;
"Yet not My will, O Father, Thine be done!"

Exhausted, bleeding, prostrate on the ground,
Down in the depths of suffering profound,
And the last tempest gathering around.

Oh! who but fated Judas could betray
Him upon whom such weight of sorrow lay?
A murderer's kiss took Jesu's life away.

Then with rough cords they bound His blessed hands,
And led Him down amidst infuriate bands;
Now before Caiaphas He meekly stands.

O sad Gethsemane! thy groans and tears
Have melted hearts through centuries of years;
And still we weep whene'er thy name appears.

O agony intense! O bloody sweat!
Gethsemane and Calvary paid my debt,
And Christ, with bleeding hands, opes heaven's gate.

In burning love I fall and kiss Thy feet,
Scourged, mocked, and bleeding—Thee, my God, I greet,
Bearing the Cross, to make my bliss complete.

CALVARY.

CLIMBING the hill of Calvary I fall
  Prostrate, and muse upon Thy grief and thrall,
  And bowing, worship Thee, Thou Lord of all.

The Man of sorrows groaned and suffered here
Unutterable anguish, pangs severe;
Bruised, wounded, smitten,—no deliverer near.

Here stood the cross, and here the maddened crowd
Mocked and blasphemed in imprecations loud,
Till their meek Victim's head in death was bowed.

Methinks, amid the stillness all around,
I hear, even now, the echoings resound
Of that dread day, when earthquakes rent the ground.

The heavens again seem darkened,—earth, sky, sea,
All blotted out, as though they ceased to be,
And only Jesus on the cross I see.

O heart! beat not so loud.   In silence deep
I view the Shepherd dying for the sheep,
And in an agony of sorrow, weep.

O sacred Head ! pierced with the cruel thorn ;
O hands and feet transfixed, and nailed, and torn ;
O Visage marred and languid, sad, and worn.

Writhing in fierce intensity of pain,
The crimson life-blood flows from every vein,
Most dear, most blessed Lord, wrung, tortured, slain

One bitter cry ! the loudest and the last,
Thrills through my inner soul, but all is past,
And the pale hues of death His face o'ercast.

My Lord ! my God ! my Jesus crucified,
Dies on the cross—but watching, I abide—
I see the Roman soldier pierce His side.

And loving Joseph comes with evening's gloom
To swathe his Lord—in bitter sorrow dumb—
With reverent hands, and lay Him in his tomb.

O Jesus ! on Mount Calvary I see
Stern justice and pure love unite in Thee ;
Thy pains and death bring endless life to me.

Lifting my eyes, I see my risen Lord
From Bethany ascend, to heaven restored ;
I hear His loving voice, His parting word.

Prayer becomes praise, and darkness melts in light,
Earth smiles again in gladness, heaven grows bright,
And men and angels in one song unite.

Climbing the hill of Calvary day by day,
Henceforth I journey on my heavenward way
With quickened step, and live to watch and pray.

To love Thee, Jesus, is my life's endeavour ;
From Thee, my all, nor life nor death shall sever ;
Body, soul, spirit, I am Thine for ever !

THE WRECK OF "THE LONDON"

(WHICH FOUNDERED IN THE BAY OF BISCAY ON HER VOYAOE TO
AUSTRALIA, JANUARY 6, 1866, WHEN ABOUT 220 PASSENOERS
AND CREW WERE DROWNED).

FROM Plymouth Harbour sailed a goodly vessel,
    Freighted full deep with cargo fore and aft ;
Boldly she went forth with the storm to wrestle,
    A grand and stately craft.

With cheery hearts the captain and his crew,
    And twelvescore passengers, the voyage begun,
And prayer commingled with the last adieu,
    When fired the midnight gun.

Over the sea the iron voyager bounded,
    Ploughing the waves as though in conscious might,
And ere the bell of the last watch resounded,
    England was out of sight.

Calm was the morning, and light breezes blowing,
    As they steamed bravely seawards through the day ;
At fifteen knots an hour, the good ship going
    Onwards made steady way.

But when the Sunday dawned, the wind, awaking
  Like a sea-giant starting from his sleep,
Rushed in a wild tornado, fiercely breaking
    The fountains of the deep.

Jibboom and top-mast, royal-mast and spars,
  Shivered and rent, were flung into the sea ;
Just at black midnight, without moon or stars,
    That dreadful sight to see.

" Turn the ship landwards under steam's high pressure ! "
  Cried the bold captain, 'midst a treacherous lull ;
But the sea quenched their fires, so the dread measure
    Of their despair was full.

Then, their deep agony no more suppressing,
  A thrill of anguish rang throughout the ship ;
And some fell on their knees, their sins confessing,
    With trembling heart and lip.

While still the hurricane, like thunder's roaring,
  Swept on in fury, unabating still,
The sternposts crash ! and mountain waves are pouring
    The fated ship to fill.

Rolling and pitching, without mast or rudder,
  The helpless vessel surges to and fro ;
Powerless to stem the torrents that withstood her
    In that sad hour of woe.

Still battling, but still sinking, at night's noon,
  With haggard faces, ghastly in despair,
Death-doomed, they gather in the ship's saloon
    And kneel in common prayer.

And prayer brought comfort, and the wild commotion
   Of grief and breaking hearts found healing balm,
Amid the frantic howlings of the ocean
      There came a blessed calm.

With solemn voice on that last dreadful morning,
   No longer able with the foe to cope,
The dauntless captain gave the fatal warning
      To all, "There is no hope!"

"Yes! there *is* hope, and deathless consolation,
   And endless peace, and sure deliverance near!"
Re-echoed a yet louder voice.*   "Salvation,
      And Christ to save is here!"

So spake God's servant in his last endeavour,
   With tears and cries beseeching all to come
To Christ for mercy, pardon now or never,
      And heaven our glorious home.

Some clasped the Pastor's knees and wept, while others—
   Husband and wife, locked in their last embrace,
And children—sisters fair, and loving brothers—
      Lay down with covered face.

But upon all there came a resignation
   Like that which once from Martyr Stephen shone;
Submissive all, while some in exultation
      Could say, "Thy will be done."

---

* The late Rev. J. D. DRAPER, Wesleyan Minister, returning to
Australia, who was indefatigable in prayer and exhortation until the
vessel went down.

Like Peter sinking, they cried, "Lord, I perish!"
  And grasped their Saviour's hand in that dark hour;
And to the tremulous came sweet hope to cherish,
    And give to weakness power.

So, 'midst those sufferers, working all observant,
  For twelve long hours the ceaseless prayer was poured;
And love's soft whisper says, "God gave His servant
    The souls of all on board."

Deeper and deeper sank the wreck, all shattered;
  Faster and faster rushed the foaming tide;
Above, below, in every corner scattered,
    The silent mourners hide.

Then, with a swirling eddy, half uplifted,
  Head foremost, plunging with a sudden throe,
The mighty vessel sunk, where she had drifted
    Into the gulf below.

But over that dark bay of storm and strife
  A voice of triumph echoes from the skies,—
"I am the Resurrection and the Life,"
    "The dead in Christ shall rise!"

And ministering angels, with their wings outspread,
  Came down from glory, all aglow with love,
And swiftly, with those ransomed ones they sped
    To heaven's sweet rest above.

EPITAPH ON AN INFANT.

 BABE in Christ lies here asleep,—
Why should his sorrowing parents weep?
The infant is an angel now,
With golden crown upon his brow.

Why should we mourn his loss, or grieve?
He lived to die, but died to live;
A tender flower just budding here,
To blossom in a brighter sphere.

Sweet babe! redeemed by blood divine,
And sealed with the baptismal sign,
How pure thy joys! how calm thy rest!
In Jesu's loving arms embraced!

𝔓art 𝔗wo.—𝔕ural 𝔓oems.

BEAUTIFUL SPRING.

COME, beautiful Spring! thy garlandry bring
   Of leafage and flowers,
  And sweet alternations of sunshine and
    showers.
Come, beautiful Spring! thy choristers bring,
  Their concert to swell
In pæans of joy over mountain and dell.

At thy coming, earth breaks forth into mirth,
  And the wintry and sad
Dissolves into smiles, and all nature is glad.
From long silent nooks, clear streamlets and brooks
  Break loose from their chains,
Leaping down from the hills, through pastures and plains.

As thy footsteps advance, there is life in thy glance
  And love in thy smile,
Which brightens our hope, and sweetens our toil.
The lily of Lent, with its head meekly bent,
  And the snowdrop so white,
With the crocus in delicate clusters unite.

Along the green lanes, where solitude reigns,
        The hedgerow is gay,
And primrose and violet their beauties display.
The winter-bound wheat springs up at thy feet,
        To welcome thee near;
And the icicle melts because thou art here.

O beautiful Spring! by peasant and king—
        In palace and cot—
Thou art welcome to all, whatever their lot.
The winter is 'past, with its hurricane blast,
        And snowdrifts and gloom,
And the time of the singing of birds is come.

Thy life-giving power unfolds every hour,
        While children in throngs
Shout welcome, in innocent laughter and songs.
O jubilant Spring! thy praises we sing!
        But rapture is awed,
For the glory of Spring is the goodness of God.

SPRING AND WINTER.

A S the month of March was ending,
    And gleams of sunshine broke,
    As though suddenly awoke,
        And scudding clouds
    Like fleecy shrouds
Were parting, and then blending,
    Sweet Spring came forth one morning,
With blooming cheeks and sparkling eyes,
Like a bright angel from the skies
    At early dawning.

Her golden hair hung loosely down
    In ringlets rare to see,
And on her head a crown
    She wore, of twining blossoms three :
Lent's earliest lily—violet sweet—
And the pale primrose there did meet,
Woven with blooming palm-branch slender,
And some green leaflets young and tender.
A bunch of snowdrops in her hand
    She holdeth,
And at her breast—fondly caressed—
    A bleating lamb she foldeth.

As she drew near,
Beneath her footsteps dear

The ice-bound river, fringed with snow,
   Melted and warmed into new life,
And straight began to flow
   With music rife,
Singing in calm content,
   Watering its banks,
Which, wheresoe'er the stream is sent,
   Blossomed in thanks.

And overhead the budding trees,
Just shaken by the breeze,
   Most beautifully glitter
With icicles, all now
   Dissolved to shining dew;
Sparkling like jewels set on Beauty's brow,
   Charming the view.
   The woodland songsters twitter,
The thrush breaks forth in song,
   The cooing dove
   Proclaims his love,
And in the mighty oaks so strong,
   Waving in majesty above,
The noisy rooks, ten thousand strong,
At the first glance of spring,
   Uproarious, but one-willed,
Stretch their black wing
   And build.

O changeful March! what darkling clouds o'erspread!
   How the wind howls! a tempest is at hand;
And grim old Winter, in a snowstorm dread,
   Comes back again, and waves his frozen wand;

Songs hush, streams stagnate, gloomy, dark, and stern ;
Winter resumes his reign, and frosty days return.

Sweet Spring retires, and hides herself awhile
   Beneath a snow drift on the southern side
Of a warm wood, which courts the virgin smile
   Of sunshine, and feels life's genial tide
     Soon as it flows.
There she awaits, in gentleness resigned,
   Bright April showers, and with the cuckoo's song
Will issue forth in loveliness refined ;
   Strewing the earth with flowers, and so prolong
Her welcome reign, till the wheat ears entwined
     Wave to the summer rose.

APRIL SHOWERS.

APRIL is like a young and passionate child,
        Beauteous, but strong of will ;
    For ever changing,—soft and mild
        As love can make her now,
With angel smiles upon her brow ;
    Anon inclined to tempers that are ill,
And weeping floods of tears.
So when this welcome month appears
She comes to our caresses,
With unbound flowing tresses,
Singing a merry tune
Of loving May and June ;
And ushered in by sunshine sweet,
The daisies spring up at her feet,
And crowned with hyacinth and primrose pale,
And followed by the nightingale.

But a cloud gathers, and her lovely face
    Frowns with dark passion's storm,
Shrouding awhile the grace
    Of her fair form.
Torrents of tears flow down,
But glittering through her frown,
A rainbow arch is spread
Over her head ;

And the clouds part asunder
With one sharp peal of thunder;
And soon the sunshine glorious
Breaks forth again victorious,
And April, flinging back her tresses,
Courts fresh caresses,
Wreathing her hair with flowers,
Wet with the genial showers.

Beautiful April! whom men call fickle,
   In changeful rainbow hues,
We love thee dearly and sincerely;
Nor should we need the harvest scythe or sickle
   But for thy showers and dews.

TO A NIGHTINGALE.

HAIL, beautiful bird ! whoever has heard
          Thy exquisite song
Will find nowhere else such a musical tongue.
Hail, wonderful bird !   Thy melody stirred
          Flows lovingly free,
And nature is hushed to listen to thee.

Creation around no rival has found ;
          In sweetness alone
Thou sittest, star-crowned, on harmony's throne.
Peacocks may unfold, all radiant with gold,
          Their fire-spangled tail ;
Still we say, " My little brown nightingale, hail ! "

Down in the lone copse, where glittering dewdrops
          Gem the point of the thorn,
Untiring thou singest from evening till morn,
In soft modulations and countless vibrations,
          Now rapid, now slow—
Impassioned, or falling as gently as snow.

When the hawthorn's in bloom, and its fragrant perfume
          On the night breezes float,
Then the nightingale pours forth her amorous note.
And in woodlands and dells all peerless she swells
          Her hymn's loftiest flight,
Like an angel sent down to sing through the night.

Hail, beautiful bird! ever since I first heard
     Thy heart-thrilling song,
I mourn that thou always art absent so long.
Thy fluttering wing just opens in spring,
     But ere midsummer dawn,
And blossom expand into fruit, thou art gone.

Methinks the pure song of thy affluent tongue
     On Nativity's morn
Was taught thee by angels, when Jesus was born.
They sang in the night, and they sang in delight,
     Like thee, thou sweet bird;
So the nightingale's dear wherever she's heard.

MOONLIGHT IN SPRING.

THE pensive moonbeams kiss the early flowers
  This lovely night,
    And their pale smile illumes the woodland
      bowers
  Of primroses, and cherry orchards white
With snowy bloom and rich with fragrance sweet.
What charms at this still hour of midnight meet
  And beautifully blend !
Bright dewy diamonds sparkle at my feet
  Numberless and without end.
A gentle breeze scarce ruffles the young leaves
  Fresh opened to the genial breath of spring ;
And nature's face a stamp receives
  Of placid joy such as spring moonlights bring.

Here a pure streamlet flows,
Making most cheerful music as it goes ;
Whether in bleak December or fair June,
This little stream is never out of tune.
But now, beneath the full moon's beam,
The nightingale outsings the stream ;
Or rather, the two songs unite,
Made richer by the hush of night.
What passion mingles in that matchless song,
Which the lone echoes of the woods prolong !

Now low, now high—or soft and faint,
As though it meekly breathed complaint.
Anon a marvellous burst of power,
   Thrilling the soul
As sudden as an April shower;
   Pouring without control,
Then gurgling from the throat
As prelude to a clear transparent note,
Drawn out, and lengthening still
At the sweet songster's will:
Earth has no music like it, strains celestial
Seem linked with songs terrestrial!

But now the windings of the carol cease
    In deep, deep peace;
And my heart feels a quietude benign,
    Which surely is divine.

THE WAYSIDE SPRING.

H, stop and drink at this beautiful spring,
  By the highway roadside flowing;
Where, in the palace of a king,
  Is a purer or brighter glowing?
Beautiful spring! for ever rife,
Winter and summer sparkling with life.

Nature has scooped out a fountain for thee,
  Skilfully sunken, deep and broad,
Gurgling and bubbling up, merry and free,
  This spring by the side of the road;
Which says, as it murmuring trails o'er the brink,
To all that pass by, "Come and drink! come and drink!"

There's a sloping bank at the back of the spring,
  Overhung by hazel and sloe,
Where the summer birds meet and joyously sing,
  And wild flowers nestle and blow;
And travellers rest in the shade of the trees,
Sung to sleep by the beautiful stream and the bees.

See the children escaping from school, blithe as May,
  Run down the hillside, glad to be free,
All to the fountain making their way;
  Some lap with their hand, some drop on their knee,

Drinking the water, then make the air ring
With shouts in praise of this beautiful spring.

Oh, stop and drink at this beautiful spring
  By the highway roadside flowing !
Health and long life its waters bring ;
  And all is God's bestowing,
Clear as the crystal, lovely and bright,
Beautiful spring of joy and delight !

THE SKYLARK.

THE lark mounts up at earliest dawn,
  With dewdrops glistening on his wings,
In hasty flight from earth withdrawn,
  And vaulting heavenward, soars and sings ;
Bathing in morning's virgin light,
And distancing the eagle's flight.

Up at heaven's gate, in notes of praise,
  The skylark sings his matin hymn ;
And when he's lost to human gaze,
  And his sweet song grows faint and dim,
Perchance he spreads his speckled wing,
Poised where the wakeful angels sing.

But now the skylark and his notes
  Are lost to hearing and to view,
And now his feathered pinion floats
  High in the bright celestial blue ;
A choral messenger from earth
Joining in songs of heavenly mirth.

But hark ! a fluttering sound I hear,
  The lark returns in downward flight ;
Again his melody is near,
  Again the chorister in sight,
With tireless wing and sparkling breast,
Drops singing to his lowly nest.

THE WOODPECKER.

SILENCE pervades the woods,
   And through their solitudes
     Not a single bird is singing.
    In the distance I can hear
Village children laugh and cheer,
   And wedding bells are ringing;
But only one sound in the wood
   Echoes, one, and only one:
Every moment 'tis renewed,
   Now again begun.

Gently tapping, quickly rapping
   On a high tree, out of reach,
The woodpecker is tapping,
While his outspread wings are flapping,
Ever rapping, sharply tapping
   At the trunk of yonder beech;
Tapping, rapping, out of reach,
At the trunk of yonder beech.

Here I'll sit down, shaded
   By overhanging boughs,
And watch this woodpecker unaided
   Excavate his high-pitched house,
Far out of danger's reach;

Quickly rapping, sharply tapping,
　　How he works,
　　And never shirks !
Labours on until he's done,
Working till the setting sun,
At his tunnel in the beech.

I begin to like the sound :
　　My woodpecker, work on !
May your house complete be found
　　Before the setting sun.
Echo still your lively tapping,
While your outspread wings are flapping
　　Far above me, out of reach ;
Working in the greenwood shade,
Working till your house is made
　　In the trunk of yonder beech.
Lonely bird, whose wings are flapping
While you still continue tapping,
Tapping, rapping, tapping, rapping,
　　At the trunk of yonder beech.

THE MOUNTAIN ASH.

HURRAH for the mountain ash !
  On the broad upland growing,
Where the earliest beams of morning flash
Through its spreading boughs, and tempests
    dash
When wintry blasts are blowing.
Oh, the mountain ash is a noble tree ;
The ash, the mountain ash for me !

Its roots strike down in the soil,
  Grasping the earth as its own ;
Firm as a rock, without trouble or toil,
It stands, and seems to say, with a smile,
  "This field is my freehold and throne ;
I'm a mountain ash, and I wear a crown,—
Where's the woodman's axe shall cut me down ?"

Its stem is as straight as a line,
  Without a knot or a bough,
Twenty yards high, with graceful decline
To the top, where branches lace and entwine,
  And in waving foliage bow
To the stormy wind or whispering breeze,
This mountain ash on the upland leas.

'Twas just fifty years ago
   My father planted this tree;
A stake and a spade he carried, I know,
And he said, " My son, with me thou shalt go,
   This mountain ash is for thee."
So on my shoulder I bore the tree,
This mountain ash, which belongs to me.

Father is long ago dead,
   And with age I am growing grey,
But this tree its mighty branches has spread,
And a flock of sheep repose in the shade
   Of this ash, planted on All Saints' day,—
Still in its prime of vigorous growth :
So this mountain ash will outlive us both.

Still in the vigour of youth
   This mountain ash is growing,
And it makes my heart sad, in sooth,
To read, deeply cut in its bark, the truth—
   " The scythe of death is mowing ;"
And to feel waning in life's decay,
While this mountain ash is strong and gay.

What matter ?   Oh, why should I mourn ?
   Those children, wreathing their flowers
On the root of the tree, may return
Half a century hence a lesson to learn,
   Like me, in life's closing hours.
And the sunset glory still may flash
Among the leaves of this mountain ash.

SONG OF A RIVULET.

I AM a little rivulet,
   And come dancing down the hill,
   Through wooded fell and stony dell,
   And always with good-will.
My home is on the mountain side,
  From a mossy bank I flow,
'Midst root and bush I brightly gush,
  And sing where'er I go.

Somewhile my course is hidden
  Beneath the tangled grass,
So I wind and turn amongst the fern,
  And merrily onward pass.
Warily creeping, or boldly leaping
  Down the falls in a cascade,
Through stately trees, where the soft breeze
  Sleeps in the brushwood shade.

In winter I'm not frozen,
  And in summer never dry;
I'm always moving, ever loving,
  Kissing all that I pass by;

The monarch oaks I cherish,
  I beget the daisy's bloom ;
Wild roses wreathe, and violets breathe
  On me their rich perfume.

And then in the fair spring-time,
  When all around is still,
And the pale moon at midnight's noon
  Shines calmly o'er the hill,
The nightingales, in concert,
  Join the little rivulet's lay,
Chanting all night, in pure delight,
  Until the break of day.

In gloomy hours or sunshine,
  Ever by day and night,
In cold or heat, my step is fleet,
  I work with all my might.
Running on, running ever,
  Clear, beautiful, and rife,
I only live to love and give
  A rivulet of life.

I am a little rivulet,
  And my home is in the wood,
But I joy to flow, and as I go
  To sing, and to do good.
My stream is clear as crystal,
  And I feed the brook below,
And flocks and herds and beasts and birds
  The little rivulet know.

I am a little rivulet,
    But many centuries old ;
Thousands of years, in joys and tears,
    O'er me, like waves, have rolled.
A rivulet among the hills,
    God made me thus to flow,
And sound His praise, in humble lays,
    And bless where'er I go.

MOONRISE.

SIT down and rest awhile
      On this low woodland stile,
      And see the full moon rise clothed in pure
            light,
   And queenly beauty, all her own.
For now, in state, she comes to rule the night,
   Upon her ancient throne,
      The queen of peace.

Her heralds are bright rays,
      Whose radiancy increase
Each moment as we gaze,
Deeper and deeper growing,
And more intensely glowing,
Silvery and faint at first,
   And softly moulden ;
Now suddenly they burst
   In glittering glory golden ;
The clouds seem all on fire,
   And the blaze spreads
Upwards, still leaping higher
   Over our heads.

And the moon's disc is seen
    Above the horizon's edge, as crystal bright,
Rising with speed, ineffably serene,
    In full-orbed light.
With one attendant satellite,
    A courtier star, I ween,
With sweet celestial will,
Shining and waiting still
    Upon Night's queen.

The distant sheep-bell echoes from the hill,
    While the lone nightingale resumes his strains;
All else is eloquently still,
    And moonlight reigns.

BIRDS OF SONG.

FREE and fearless soar along,
  Beautiful, beautiful birds of song!
  Bright of eye, and swift of wing,
  Through the blue sky wandering;
Scorning sorrow, care, and thrall,
Ever richly musical.

Onwards in your bright career,
  Beautiful birds of song,
Breathe not a note that tells of fear,
  As ye wildly speed along.
Over the hills in verdure clad,
Your melody 'tis that maketh glad,
Over the valleys, gay with corn,
Ye warble a matin-song at morn.
Where is the hand would do you wrong,
Beautiful, beautiful birds of song?

Let the eagle mount up when the storm has done,
And spread abroad his wings in the sun,
Let him build his eyry, lonely and proud,
On the pinnacled rock which pierces the cloud,
Cleaving the heavens with star-bright eye,
And basking in infinity's sky;
The eagle is noble, majestic, and free,
But the birds of song are dearer to me.

When the gentle spring beams on the earth,
Who, who awakes the carol of mirth?
Who singeth in concert with running streams,
Mingling their music with our dreams?
Whose notes across the summer glade
Murmur in dirges as the flowers fade,
Lingering until autumn dies,
And winter's hurricanes sweep through the skies?
'Tis the singing birds, the choral throng,
The beautiful, beautiful birds of song!

THE EARLY THRUSH.

THE thrush sings in the leafless tree
    In earliest spring,
And with his buoyant melody
    The woodlands ring.
Sweet thrush! whose cheerful music flows
Before we lose the winter's snows.

Soon as the storm-clouds break and whiten
    In fleecy smile,
And flashing sunbeams burst and brighten
    The earth awhile,
Sweet thrush! thy cheerful music flows
Before the virgin snowdrop blows.

At early morn, when o'er the hills
    Daylight appears,
Thy song the ear of morning fills,
    And nature cheers.
Sweet thrush! the winter drear and lóng
Is shortened by thy welcome song.

In some lone bush or stunted tree
    Thy nest is found,
Ere the green sheltering leaves we see,
    Or flowers abound.
Sweet thrush! who singest to thy mate
Within her nest, early and late.

Before the cuckoo and the swallow,
    Or nightingale,
Skim o'er the hill and hollow,
    Or blooming vale,
Sweet thrush! thy mellow tones are heard,
The first of any singing bird.

Thou singest till the stars appear,
    And the moon's beam
Shines faintly, and thy notes are clear
    As running stream;
Sweet thrush! from the tall ash or lime
We love to hear thy warbling chime.

With speckled breast, and buoyant wing,
    And eye of light,
We call thee, as thy praise we sing,
    "The spring's delight."
Sweet thrush! who in the dawning year
Sings, long before the flowers appear.

A SEA-SIDE CALM.

THE sea is calm and glassy as a lake
    Unruffled, slumbering on in deep repose,
Whose gentle undulations hardly break
    In ripples as it flows.

And bright as calm, in ceaseless variation
    Of ever-beautiful but changing hues,
Rising and falling, like a soft pulsation,
    Which every breath renews.

And glittering in the sunbeams, clearly shining,
    A slanting line of radiance spreads afar
To where the ocean seems asleep, reclining,
    Beyond the tidal bar.

The tide is flowing in, but comes so meekly,
    Kissing the pebbles on the shingly beach,
Like the first steps of childhood, shy and weakly,
    Or the first lisping speech.

And yonder, in the offing, ships and boats,
    Alike becalmed, lie waiting for the gale
With drooping pennons, while the sea-bird floats
    Idly, with frequent wail.

How silent, yet how beautiful the scene!
　　Sweet emblem of the soul's repose in God;
The joy unruffled, and the peace serene,
　　　　On humble souls bestowed.

And as just now the setting sun sinks down,
　　As though he sank embosomed on the sea,
So may I find in death my bliss, my crown
　　　　Of life, O God, in Thee!

A SEA-SIDE STORM.

HARK! how the ocean roars! may Heaven
defend us
From the wild fury of the maddened waves;
Foaming and surging, terribly tremendous,
The angry tempest raves.

Heaving and groaning, as in giant throes,
Rising and falling, uncontrolled and grand,
The yesty billows only find repose
By breaking on the strand.

See yonder ship—already half a wreck,
Struck by the waves, dismantled by the shock;
A hundred hapless mariners on deck,
Dashed on the treacherous rock.

Hurled landwards by the wind-lashed torrent's power,
High on the billows, with tumultuous roar,
Vessel and crew and cargo, in an hour,
Are flung upon the shore.

Thunders are rolling, and the lightnings' flashing
Adds tenfold terror to the dreadful scene;
Broken to shivers, hear the timbers crashing,
Sad shrieks of woe between.

Amidst the massy boulders crushed and battered,
  Living and dead commingle in their woe ;
O luckless ship ! O heart-brave sailors shattered,
    And thus in death laid low !

The storm-bird screams, and still the storm increases,
  Mountain on mountain-billows rend in spray,
As though they'd cleave the granite cliff in pieces,
    And tear the land away.

Be still, O tempest !   He that on the Lake
  Of Galilee, amidst the storm's commotion,
Cried, " Peace ! " and waves obeyed Him when He spoke,
    Still rules the ocean.

Omnipotent in royalty divine,
  He reigns supreme, and governs sea and land ;
Peace, boisterous ocean ! ever held within
    The hollow of His hand.

Night falls, and yonder from her foamy bed
  The full moon rises with a placid brow ;
Was ever moonlight on the ocean shed
    More beautiful than now ?

COME AGAIN, SWEET SPRING.

 COME again, sweet Spring,
    With thy gush of joy and love,
Bright glance and rainbow wing,
    And odours from above.
Come again with thy sunny hours,
    Clear morn and balmy even ;
Come with thy garlandry of flowers,
    And songs that breathe of heaven.

Come with thy cheeks fresh beaming
    With a pure and healthful hue ;
Come with thy ringlets streaming,
    Like tendrils in the dew.
Come with thy murmuring rivers,
    And thy tuneful streamlets bring,
And the nestling bird that quivers,—
    O come again, sweet Spring.

Come again with thy sunrise splendour,
    And the glories of mid-day ;
Come with thy radiance tender,
    When moonlight melts away.
Come in the showers which glitter
    Like diamonds as they fall ;
Come with sweet birds which twitter
    Their woodland madrigal.

Come with thy primroses,
   And violets' lovely hue ;
Pale daffodils and roses,
   And hyacinths of blue ;
Thy hedgerows bright with wild flowers,
   And gardens in full bloom ;
The cherry orchard's blossom,
   And the apple tree's perfume.

Come with thy scented gales,
   Gay fields, and peasants haying ;
Come with thy nightingales,
   And merry children Maying.
Art thou angry, that so long
   Thou art spreading forth thy wing ?
Come in full beauty and full song,
   O come again, sweet Spring.

THE WILD ROSE.

THE rose! the wild, wild rose!
　　In vernal beauty drest;
　　Where music-warbling streamlet flows,
　　And woodlands wave in calm repose,
　　There, there thy bloom is best.
In boyhood's hour this gentle flower
　　Oft crowned my childish glee;
And even now for beauty's brow,
Sweet blossom, what so fair as thou?
　　The wild, wild rose for me.

The rose! the wild, wild rose!
　　I love its maiden hue;
Rich is the fragrance which it throws
Around, when morning's sunrise glows,
　　And gems its tears of dew.
Let others prize carnation-dyes,
　　And never dream of thee;
My humble lays of ardent praise,
Sweet blossom, I will ever raise,—
　　The wild, wild rose for me.

WILD HYACINTHS.

'TWAS in the merry month of May,
   When spring is gaily drest,
   I saw, beside the public way,
   A woodland copse in rich array,
  Facing the genial west;
Filled with wild hyacinths in bloom,
Breathing around their sweet perfume.

All o'er the copse the flowers were spread,
   Most beautiful to view,
Waving before the breeze, and fed
By April showers and sunshine shed,
   And ever-sparkling dew,
Which glittered in ten thousand drops,
Like jewels in that lovely copse.

A murmuring stream ran down the vale,
   And in a whitethorn tree,
In snowy bloom, the nightingale
Poured forth his song, as if to hail
   Those wild flowers bright and free;
Those hyacinths' imperial blue,
Waved by the loving breeze which blew.

Oft in my dreams those million flowers—
  An acre all in bloom—
Are freshened by the vernal showers,
Or blossom in May's sunny hours,
  And scatter their perfume;
While every passing traveller stops
To view those hyacinths in the copse.

MAY FLOWERS.

FLOWERS! flowers! beautiful flowers!
    Everywhere flowers!
    In fields and in woods, and festooning in
        bowers,
Flowers! flowers! beautiful flowers!
The birds are merrily singing,
And the May-day bells are ringing,
And the soft south wind is blowing,
And the bright sunshine glowing
From the clear sky above,
Cloudless, and warm with love.
The children are out Maying,
    Bright as the day,
Garlands displaying,
    In honour of May-day.
All the flowers of early spring
On this joyous day they bring;
Wild flowers and garden flowers,
Nursed in the April showers,
Flowers! flowers! beautiful flowers!
    Everywhere flowers!
In fields and in woods, and festooning in bowers,
Flowers! flowers! beautiful flowers!

Now ramble with me Maying
    Down this green lane,
Boughs overhead are swaying
    To the wind's gentle strain,
Whispering calm music to the ear,
That nature's harmonies can hear.
    Stand still and look
At this small wayside nook,
Whence floats a waft of fragrance on the breeze,
    From violets blue and white,
        Hidden from sight,
Blooming among the roots of trees ;
To virtue's solitude allied,
Unseen they blow, but spread their odours wide.
So this wild thyme, with aromatic scent,
    Perfumes the air,
And hyacinths and cowslips blent,
    In company are there.
On both sides of the way
    Primroses smile and cluster,
And the wild tulip and the oxlip gay
    Are in full lustre.
The wood-anemone, which shuns the cold,
    Closing at night,
To-day shines out in white and gold,
    Glad of the sunny light.
Flowers ! flowers ! beautiful flowers !
    Everywhere flowers !
In fields and in woods, and festooning in bowers,
Flowers ! flowers ! beautiful flowers !

Now to the fields and woods,
Creation's solitudes

With flowers are gay
Always on this sweet day,
The pastures glitter in their rainbow vest,
   And buttercups of golden hue
Mingle with the musk-mallow's purple crest,
   And the forget-me-not's pale blue.
The common furze, for evermore in bloom,
   Enlivens hedge and copse ;
And here and there I see a cheerful broom
   On the bleak upland tops.
The woods are redolent of sweets
   Within their lone domain,
   Where solitude and beauty reign ;
And wildest wild flowers in their safe retreats
Blossom from year to year.
Nature's own temple in the woods is here,
And here the breathing incense of her flowers,
Through spring and summer, and autumnal hours,
Ascends to heaven in worship undefiled.
   The woods are choristers, for ever singing,
     Touching the harp-strings of the pliant trees,
To music grand and wild ;
    And heavenly melodies
  Are upward winging.

Gather the wild flowers in the woods,
   And join creation's lay ;
God's smile is in these solitudes,
   His smile is May.
Down from the hills with garlands come,
Gather the flowers in bloom ;
When God gives joy,
O let not man or sin alloy.

Flowers ! flowers ! beautiful flowers !
   Everywhere flowers !
In fields and in woods, and festooning in bowers,
Flowers ! flowers ! everywhere flowers !
Flowers ! flowers ! beautiful flowers !

CONSIDER THE LILIES.

CONSIDER the field lilies, how they grow,
Watered by crystal brooklets as they flow
Through verdant pastures, singing as they
go.

They neither toil nor spin ; no friendly hand
Trains them in growing, yet their leaves expand,
And their fair flowers in glowing clusters stand.

The gentle rain, with influence benign,
Falls on their opening blossoms, and suns shine
Upon them with a quickening power divine.

How exquisitely beautiful and white !
Charming at once to scent and fair to sight !
God's lilies are they, sent for man's delight.

Consider them, these lilies, made to please,
So rich that Solomon, in pomp and ease,
Was never yet arrayed like one of these.

Like virgin bridesmaids in their veils of snow,
Young, pure, and innocent, no care or woe
These chaste and spotless lilies ever know.

Waving in quiet beauty all your own,
Ye teach a lesson worthy being known—
Of calm content, and trust in God alone.

O lilies of the field ! from you I learn
The Christly lesson, sin and pride to spurn,
In modest goodness won, and meekly worn.

THE HILLS OF KENT.

THE hills of Kent, the hills of Kent,
  How beautiful they are !
Like green Arcadian lands of song,
  Or Italy afar.
Swathed in their robe of summer bloom,
  And leafage fair and bright,
They slumber in the sunny beam,
  And glow in summer light.
Adown their vernal bosoms throb
  A thousand crystal veins,
Outpouring living melody
  Along the fertile plains ;
And mingling with the Medway deep,
  Which calmly glides along
With silvery tide, that whispered once
  To classic Sydney's song.

The hills of Kent, the hills of Kent,
  I love to see them lie
In still repose when morning streaks
  With fire the eastern sky,
When slowly from the far-off vale
  Uprolls the river mist,
And every flower and wind-swept mead
  By dewy lips is kissed.

'Tis sweet at noontide's sultry hour,
　　Nor less when evening fades,
With rainbow flush and tremulous sigh,
　　In milder moonlight shades,
To watch the glance of dying day,
　　The gentle night-bird near,
Till rich elysian music breaks
　　In chorus on the ear.

The hills of Kent, the hills of Kent,
　　Upon whose summits stand
The rustic cottage, and the halls
　　Of those who rule the land ;
The village church, all ivy-clad,
　　With bells and rugged spire,
Where pure devotion's anthems rise,
　　And warm the rural choir ;
The homes of love with plenty crowned,
　　The fields and orchards wide,
The hop-gardens' mild fragrance,
　　And the flocks, the farmers' pride.
Where'er I rove my memory turns,
　　And echoes from afar,
The hills of Kent, the hills of Kent,
　　How beautiful they are !

EARLY IN JUNE.

A LONG the green lanes wandering,
　　Early in June,
　Where a clear stream meandering,
　　Always in tune,
Sings ever as it flows,
　Unchecked, unbidden,
'Midst garlands of wild rose
And blooming briar; on it goes,
　Still singing, seen or hidden;
On either bank flowers cluster,
Aglow with life and lustre,
　In festoons wreathing,
　Rich odours breathing;
And bending willows, and tall trees
　Of centuries' growth,
Stretch their long arms to meet the breeze,
And flourish, watered by the stream.
This little, merry, dancing stream,
Which men may useless deem,
　Gives life to both.
Sweet crystal stream, for ever moving,
　　And every flower caressing,
　Like thee, by gentleness made great,
May I be working, singing, loving,
　Content in low estate,
　　Blessèd and blessing,

A little stream, amidst the strife
  Of this bad world, ever in tune,
And flowing towards the sea of life,
Good, and with goodness rife ;
Like thee, meandering stream,
Chanting where poets dream
  Early in June.
The summer sun is shining
  Early in June,
And overhead entwining,
The mighty oaks combining,
  Give shelter cool at noon.
Like pillars reared on either hand,
See God's cathedral stand,
  Simple yet grand ;
Roofed with umbrageous boughs,
  In glittering sheen,
And lit with sunshine bright,—
Radiant with light
  And summer green.

Here pay thy morning vows,
Along the green lanes wandering
  Early in June ;
Out of thy heart's deep pondering
  Sing some old tune
Sung in thy youthful days ;
  Lift up thy soul,
And yield to Heaven's control
Beneath this living roof, and on this sod
  Shout forth God's praise,—
This is God's temple, here is God !

The running stream reminds us
  To be always up and doing,
That every day may find us
  Some good pursuing.
The scented flowers teach duty,
Linked evermore with beauty,
That men may be enticed
By love, to love and follow Christ.
And the tall trees o'erspreading,
  Like roof of minster nave,
That at each step we're treading
  Upon a neighbour's grave,—
These lessons learnt we wandering,
  One short forenoon,
Beside a stream meandering,
  Early in June.

THE BEAUTIFUL BROOK.

COME and look, come and look at the
        beautiful brook,
        Flowing for ever, flowing for miles
        Along the valley in midsummer smiles ;
Clear as the crystal of morning's light,
Glittering by day and shining by night,—
O come and look at the beautiful brook.

This beautiful brook comes down from the hills,
And its waters set going the wheels of the mills ;
Streamlets and rivulets bring the supply,
'Tis fed from the hills and the clouds of the sky.
This brook has been flowing for time out of mind,
For health and for wealth in blessings combined,—
O come and look at the beautiful brook.

It curves and it winds as it runs on its way,
Skirting the green woods in summer array,
Watering the garden of the cotter's abode,
Close by the church and under the road,
Spanned by a bridge, onward it goes,
Summer and winter, onward it flows,—
O come and look at the beautiful brook.

Sweetly it flows, calmly it goes,
'Midst winterly storms or summer repose;
On its breast the white water-lily is seen,
Rushes and reeds upspringing between,
And aspen and willow lovingly seem
Drooping their boughs to drink of the stream,—
O come and look at the beautiful brook.

The swallow skims over the face of the brook,
And the kingfisher builds in some shelterèd nook,
And the water-fowls have their nest in the edge
Of the copse, 'midst the flags and the sedge;
And the sparkling trout, all spotted with gold,
Leaps when the glories of evening unfold,—
O come and look at the beautiful brook.

On the banks of the brook the valley is crowned
With blossoms, and verdure and plenty abound;
Song-birds and flowers their beauties combine,
Fields for the sheep and pastures for kine;
So the stream runs, and sings as it goes,
To nourish and bless wherever it flows,—
O come and look at the beautiful brook,
    Come and look, come and look
    At this beautiful brook.

BEFORE SUNRISE.—THE SKYLARK,

THE lark is heavenward winging
 His flight at earliest dawn,
Still soaring upwards, singing
 His welcome to the morn;
With simple strains, yet tender,
 He meets the coming day,
Before the sunrise spendour
 Has smiled the night away.

The orient star of morning
 Still glitters in the sky,
To watch the day's returning,
 And see the shadows fly;
The moon her light is paling,
 But lingers on her way,
To hear the skylark hailing
 The new-born light of day.

The reddening sky is glorious,
 The golden lustre spreads,
And Day, o'er Night victorious,
 His royal radiance sheds;
The bees begin their humming,
 The song-birds plume their wings,
But while the sun is coming
 The lark still soars and sings.

Sweet birds ! so early waking
   Thy song of praise to sing,
The summer dewdrops shaking,
   Like diamonds, from thy wing ;
The sunrise wakes a chorus
   Of birds we love to hear,
But the skylark's carol o'er us
   Is ever fresh and dear !

SUMMER MORNING.

CLUSTERING round my window, roses red
    and white,
    In beautiful profusion open to the light,
    Gracefully entwining on this summer day,
While the sun is shining with his earliest ray,—

Shining in my window, on this glorious morn,
Shining on the roses, shining on the corn;
All creation's waking, lovely as of yore,
Golden smiles are breaking as the clock strikes four.

Opening now my window, the odoriferous breathing
Of morning fills my chamber, while the roses wreathing
Round my trellised casement, swayed by the soft breeze,
Seem to say, "For this we bloom, sight and scent to please."

Underneath my window are jessamines and pinks,
And the fragrant lavender the dew of morning drinks;
While roses, all commingling, gay and brilliant shine,   .
Roses round my window lovingly entwine.

Clustering round my window, roses red and white
Waft their sweet perfuming; so thrilled with calm delight,
I sing kneeling at my bedside, with soul and body's
    powers,
"Praise God for sunshine! praise God for flowers!"

SWEET SUMMER DAY.

SWEET summer day ! I saw thee dawn
  In golden glory from the east ;
The morning star had not withdrawn,
  Nor yet the night-bird's warblings ceased.
The sun rose up in flaming might,
  While all creation owned his sway,
And glowed with throbs of new delight,
  To welcome thee, sweet summer day !

Sweet summer day ! fields, pastures, woods,
  Wild hedgerows, and the running brooks,
And far-off moorland solitudes,
  And unfrequented forest nooks,
All feel thy presence, and thy smile
  Brings life with every sunny ray,—
The husbandman's reward for toil
  Comes with thy light, sweet summer day !

Sweet summer day ! whose air is health ;
  Sweet summer clouds, and gentle rain ;
Broad acres, ripening in their wealth
  Of bending orchards and rich grain.
Grandly the sun sinks in the west,
  And slowly daylight melts away.
O man ! so bountifully blest,
  Thank God for this sweet summer day !

ROWING UP THE RIVER.

ROWING up the river on a summer day,
　　Where green aspens quiver among new-
　　　mown hay ;
　　Up the river rowing when the water's clear,
　　And the sunshine's glowing sparkles far
　　　and near.

On our oars reclining, we see, down below,
Golden trout are shining, darting to and fro ;
Fish by thousands mingle in the crystal deeps,
Mid the shells and shingle where the sunlight sleeps.

Rowing onwards stilly, with a gentle stroke,
See the water-lily, which has just awoke
From long months of dreaming, quickened into life
By the sun's warm beaming—all with beauty rife.

Now, an angle rounding, a waterfall appears,
Dashing, foaming, bounding, with its spray of tears,
From the tops of mountains, rivulets and rills,
And earth's hidden fountains, pouring from the hills.

Yonder, where its billows smooth their snowy crest,
Underneath the willows and in eddies rest,
Nightingales and thrushes join their melting lay,
And swans, among the rushes, in royal beauty stay.

Rowing up the river on a summer day,
Where green aspens quiver among new-mown hay ;
Rowing up the river, nature's song be ours,—
Praise to God, the Giver of summer fruits and flowers.

THE LINNET.

THE linnet is a merry bird;
　　When summer's smile is brightest,
Whatever songster may be heard,
　　The linnet's song is lightest.
Hark! from yon blooming hawthorn bush,
What cheerful strains of music gush!

The linnet's nest is in the gorse,
　　Five speckled eggs are in it;
That's why he makes such soft discourse
　　To please his lady linnet,
Who sits in patience, day and night,
Till five young linnets see the light.

Could I decipher what he says,
　　And to Queen's English turn it,
Doubtless 'tis love, and loving things,—
　　We might do well to learn it;
And husbands serenade their wives,
Like linnets, all their married lives.

Sing on unto thy lady-love,
　　Thou gallant little linnet;
Sing on, such tender tones must move,
　　And melt the heart, and win it.
Still let thy streaming music gush,
Sweet linnet, from the hawthorn bush.

TWO SONNETS.

ON A HILL-TOP.

COME, climb with me this hill-side ; on the top
　　You'll gain a glorious view of land and sea,
　Thousands of acres waving with their crop
　　Of ripening corn.   The sweet variety
Of fields and foliage, all in summer sheen,
　And pastures dotted o'er with flocks of sheep
And herds of cattle.   What a lovely scene
　Opens before us !   See the river creep
In silence, like a silvery line of light,
　To where the ships lie in yon ocean bay,
And the wide world of water is in sight.
O broad expanse of land ! O wondrous sea !
Here will we sing, O Lord, a psalm of praise to Thee.

IN A WOOD.

HOW the wind sings among these stately trees !
　　A deep and solemn yet harmonious bass.
　Varied by undertones—like hum of bees—
　　Rising and sinking as the breezes pass
Through the low undergrowth of bush and grass.
'Tis Nature's choral service—woodland notes
　Of self-taught melody—a concert wild,
Which on the wing of heavenly music floats,
　The litany of worship undefiled
By art or man's device—the hymn of praise
To God, which woods and trackless forests ever raise—
　The hallelujah chorus of all lands,
And in one language, since Time's earliest days,
　When waving trees by millions shout and clap their
　　hands.

UNDER THE CLIFF.

UNDER the cliff, where shadows rest in soft
    repose,
    I love to lie, when summer's golden sunshine
    glows.
Above my head, o'erhanging, in angles sharp and stiff,
Reaching halfway to the clouds, I see the wondrous cliff.

Far out of reach, some blue flowers smiling from their
    gloom,
And the scent of marjoram and thyme waft rich perfume;
And higher up the plovers and sea-birds build their nest,
And perch upon some jutting crag, or flying, seem to rest.

Upon the headland bluff oxen are grazing,—
Tremendous height! my eyesight is strained by gazing;
And a flock of sheep beside them, quietly feeding
On the summit of the cliff, no danger heeding.

But the sea is breaking silence under the cliff,
And the rising tide is bringing in a very tiny skiff;
Driven towards the shallows, she drops her anchor near,
And the merry ring of voices is welcome to my ear.

And a joyous party, landing under the cliff,
Spring gaily on the pebbles from their pretty little skiff;
So of the ever-fragrant weed I'll take a quiet whiff,
And, unseen, share their pleasure beneath the shadowy clift.

LYING ON THE SHORE.

N this calm summer day,
　　Down in a quiet bay,
　　And lying on the shore
　　　Where shells and shingle
　And seaweeds mingle,
I hear the distant roar
　Of the incoming ocean tide,
Drawing nearer and yet nearer,
Speaking louder, stronger, clearer,
Rolling, surging, breaking,
And the land echoes waking,
　Till bursting at my side
In foam and spray
On this calm summer's day.

I hear along the beach
The sea-birds screech,
And the gulls flap their wings,
　Lazily floating overhead,
While the wild oxbird springs
　Up from his pebbly bed,
With a shrill whistle of delight,
And swift and sudden flight.
Now the waves touch high-water mark,
And yonder comes a fishing bark
　Into the silent bay,
Laden with fish, for many a dainty dish,
　On this calm summer day.

O wondrous sea !
On this calm summer day
  So beautiful and free,
From this small bay
The bright waves glitter in the sun,
  Seawards for miles,
Gorgeous in ambery gold and dun ;
And sunshine lights the spray
  With rainbow smiles.

  O wondrous sea !
Thou art not always as I see thee now,
  Kissed by the timorous breeze ;
  Majestic, but at ease,
Without one darkling frown upon thy brow.
  From this lone bay
I would make friends with thee to-day
Could I but trust thee,
Smooth and gentle sea !
To glide upon thy bosom far away,
And know thee in thy trackless deeps,
Where solitude for ever keeps
Watch o'er thy fathomless domain
And chronicles thy reign,
  O wondrous sea !
Speaking kind words to me,
And rippling at my feet,
  As if to greet
My visit to this quiet bay
On this calm summer day.

THE HURRICANE.

O-NIGHT the sunset was a conflagration,
　　As though a hundred cities were on fire,
　　Blazing to midheaven in red constellation
　　　And flaming vengeance dire.

Sure prelude of the hurricane's awaking,
　　And the unbridled passion of the wind
Let loose in furious might and terror shaking,
　　And leaving wrecks behind.

First came a gusty, intermittent howling,
　　As though the hurricane would try its power,
And sullen clouds from the south-west rose, scowling
　　With black and ominous lour.

Not long the freshening tornado dallies,
　　But onward sweeps with giant rush and roar
Over the hills and plains—along the valleys,
　　On to the ocean shore.

The monarch oak soon falls, its branches crashing,
　　Five centuries old, but overthrown at last ;
And forest trees are shivered by its dashing,
　　Like straws before the blast.

What can withstand its fury? swifter, stronger,
   Destruction flying on with outspread wings
From town to city, fiercer, wider, longer,
     A greater woe it brings!

Houses are roofless soon, affrighted people
   Run for their lives, and cry to God for aid,
While here we see a tower and there a steeple
     In shapeless ruin laid.

Still the storm thickens, and the rain down-pouring
   Swells and o'erflows the rivers in their course;
And the wild winds shriek to the waters roaring,
     While both unite their force.

Does the earth tremble? we behold in wonder,
   While lightning blazes and loud thunder roars,
As though each clap would rend the hills asunder,
     And hurl them on the moors.

O wind! relentless in thy work of ruin,
   Where'er I follow thee in thy dread flight,
I trace thee in wild havoc; Death is doing
     Thy bidding this sad night.

Down to the river! all its banks are flooded,
   And the bridge swept away, and vessels lost,
The harbour is with shattered wrecks bestudded,
     And frail barks tempest-tost.

Down to the sea-side! broken ships lie shivered,
   And waves like mountains frown in angry foam,
Quenching all hope, for none can be delivered
     Until a calm shall come.

O wind! I trace thy path, with terror shrinking,
　　Walking the mighty sea, and hold my breath;
Vessel driven against vessel, crushing, sinking,—
　　A carnival of death.

The shore is strewn with wrecks, and living, dying,
　　Are all commingled in one common woe!
Hush, wind! and listen to the mariners' crying,
　　　O let thy victims go!

Ah, dost thou listen, O deceitful wind!
　　Dropped to the semblance of a summer gale;
Strangely the fierce and gentle thus combined
　　　Make me in fear turn pale.

Like a stern conqueror after fire and slaughter,
　　Thou walkest on the field among the slain;
Thy foe is routed, and I hear thy laughter,
　　　Thou dreaded hurricane!

THE SCARLET PIMPERNEL.

WHENE'ER the scarlet pimpernel so tiny
    Opens its modest blossom to the sun,
It brings good news of weather clear
        and shiny,
    A summer day begun.

Early in June, and on to mild September,
    When the blue sky is cloudless, this small flower
Blooms, and the peasant fails not to remember
    It closes to the shower.

The village maiden seeks the certain token
    When upon pleasure her young heart is set,
And says, " My pimpernel has never broken
    His word of promise yet."

The farmer, when he spies amongst the stubble
    This true barometer, so welcome, come,
Rejoicing in deliverance from trouble,
    Prepares for harvest-home.

If but the little pimpernel is blowing,
    The joyous husbandman no longer grieves,
But every hand and every team is going
    To gather in the sheaves.

So, like this simple wild flower, ever proving
    A pledge of sunshine, and a living joy,
Be my life bright with golden deeds of loving,
    Made pure from sin's alloy.

NCE in my summer rambles,
   Through underwood and brambles
I bent my way, beneath the wood's cool
    cover,
  Along an unfrequented road ;
Where ringdoves, cooing, hover,
And squirrels spring from tree to tree,
   The woodpecker's abode
   And solitary raven's home,
   Where foxes love to roam
In silence, undisturbed and free.

A little streamlet, running down the hill
In devious windings, went on singing still,
Clear as the crystal of a diamond's lustre,
   For ever shining, pure and undefiled,
As innocent simplicities which cluster
   And sparkle in a good and loving child.

A nightingale was warbling, soft and clear,
Just where a fallen tree athwart the stream,
   By some strong tempest laid,
   Had formed a natural cascade ;
So the stream sang, and then the bird,—
Was ever such rare concert heard ?
   Surpassing poet's dream.
   Sweet nightingale ! sweet stream !

I traced the trailing streamlet to its source
 On the hill-top, beneath ancestral trees ;
There the small rivulet began its course
 Of gentleness and peace.
Over my head, entwined
Wild flowers of varied kind
Formed a cool arbour, and some massive stones,
Deep bedded in the mossy bank below,
 Shaped to a fountain, always full
Of the pure waters which for ever flow,
Whispering in breezy tones
 Monotonous, but never dull.

Sweet streamlet, issuing from thy quiet home
 Up in the woods, unvisited and lone,
And lost at last in the great ocean's foam,
How art thou blessing all along thy way,
 Known or unknown !
Kissing the flowers, and cherishing day by day
 Bird, beast, and creeping thing ;
The roots of the tall oak and beech
 Are nurtured from this spring,
And pastures, far as eye can reach,
 Thy praises-sing.

Clear mountain streamlet, ever flowing
 From thy calm solitude
Up in the woods, and ever going
 Thy daily journey to do good.

OUT IN THE MEADOWS.

UT in the meadows, when the summer's lustre
　　Brightens the pastures with unnumbered
　　flowers
Smiling beneath the sunshine, as they cluster,
　　Or drinking in the showers.

Hark ! how the children shout !　That merry group
　　Are gathering hedge-flowers,—full of childish joy
Their ringing laughter, and their echoing whoop
　　Is free from care's alloy.

Along the highway the wild rose is wreathing
　　With wood clematis, beautifully fair,
And daisies, hyacinths, and cowslips breathing
　　Aroma on the air.

This placid river, running on for ever
　　In calm quiescence, but with blessings rife,
Seems to flow only with one kind endeavour
　　To give and nourish life.

And yonder in the eddy, where the mallows
　　And white and yellow lilies lift their head,
The cows stand cooling in the welcome shallows,
　　Beneath the aspen's shade.

And there a rank of stalwart labourers, mowing,
   Sweep into fragrant swathes the yielding grass ;
A dozen scythes, with rapid strokes, are going,
    As through the field we pass.

Here the fresh hay is gathered on the waggon,
   And sends its rich perfumes upon the gale,
While the tired rustics from a mighty flagon
    Drink of their home-brewed ale.

And overhead the buoyant lark is singing
   In the glad sunshine of unclouded light,—
Higher and higher rising, and still winging
    His ever-upward flight.

Out in the meadows ! take the children Maying
   While flowers are blossoming, and birds in song ;
They love to join the peasants in their haying,
    And romp the hay among.

Out in the meadows ! soon your slow pulsation
   Of love and life will feel a quickening power,—
God speaks in all the beauties of creation,
    God paints the humblest flower.

Out in the meadows ! while God spreads before us
   His summer glories, streaming from above,
Oh, add your grateful hymn to Nature's chorus,
    And love Him for His love.

LYING ON THE CLIFF.

N a bright afternoon
    In ever-lovely June,
        On the cliff-top reclining,
            Upgazing to the pure blue sky,
Cloudless, in summer lustre shining,
    Sunlit—immeasurably high,
Illimitable,—with its clear light
Dazzling my sight.

Can I now see beyond the stars,
Where Venus glows, or Mars,
Or comets rush in fiery cars
    Through the trackless infinite ?
Hush ! what is that sound which fell on my ear
    Like a stray note from heaven above ?
Is it an angel's song which I hear,
    Warm with an angel's love ?

Oh, the breeze is fresh scented with flowers,
    And the air grows purer, I deem ;
I have been lying entranced for hours
    In a beautiful dream.
Are the ties of earth all riven,
And earth changed for heaven ?
Am I dwelling in Eden's fair abode,
Radiant with God ?

That must be a swallow twittering high overhead,
　　And a sea-gull swims on the edge of the cliff;
And yonder, with white sails outspread
　　On the smooth sea, is a skiff
Drifting slowly ahead.
And the flag flies on the castle tower,
And the old church clock is striking the hour,—
One, two, three, four, five, six, seven !
So it is earth, earth still,
Not Eden, or heaven !

And the mighty cliff shadows loom
A mile on the waves, for evening is come,
And the sun gilds the brow of the distant hill,
　　Gloriously sinking ;
And it seems exquisitely still,
　　As though all Creation was thinking
Why angels are happier than men,
And whether millennium is coming, and when !

Half down the cliff is a blackthorn in bloom,
　　Breathing its odours on the air ;
And a small copse of yellow broom,
　　Glowing in yellow blossoms fair.
A nightingale on each is singing,
　　One answering the other's song,
And their harmony is ringing
　　The cliff and vale along.
Was ever song so soft and moving,
Or lovers half so loving ?
Melting in overwhelming sweetness
All melody in full completeness;

For ever changing time and tone,
Varying, but still in beauty one;
Ravishing heart and ear,—
Inimitably pure and clear.

Down from the cliff descending,
    I seek the haunts of men again;
And hark ! with rhapsody ill blending,
    The whistle of the train !
And a voice met my ear, which said,
"Do you not think that you did wrong,
Lying upon the cliff so long ?"

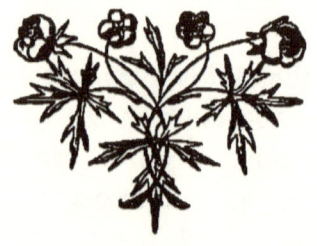

SWEET LILY OF THE VALLEY.

SWEET lily of the valley,
    Beside the streamlet growing,
    Amidst the reeds and rushes
      In modest beauty blowing;
Fenced round by delicate leaves,
Which nature interweaves,
  This welcome flower
  To the Spring shower
Comes forth in suowy sheen
Of virgin white and verdant green,
  Drooping its gentle head
Meekly, and innocently shy,
But breathing fragrance to the earth and sky,
  By gentle breezes spread.
Sweet lily of the valley,
We hail thy lowly bloom!
  By lonely brook
  For thee we look,
Scenting thy rich perfume;
  Thou welcome flower
  Of Spring's bright hour,
Sweet lily of the valley!

Sweet lily of the valley!
  The peasant on the moor
Transplants thee in thy fragrance
  To his own cottage door;

And the brow of beauty, glowing
With diamonds rare,
   More brightly shines
   When it entwines
And braids among its jewelled hair
The lily blossom there.
   On the Queen's throne
   This flower is known
'Midst pearls and rubies blazing;
   This little flower
   From rural bower,
Born of the sunshine and the shower,
Is shown for courtiers' gazing.
Baptized in morning dew,
It charms the view
Alike of high and low,
This virgin lily, white as snow.

Sweet lily of the valley!
   We praise thee, modest flower;
Thy stainless purity be ours,
Richest of priceless dowers.
And, like thy odorous sweet
In goodness all complete
   And living power,
May gentle charities combine
   With tender hearts renewed,
And our lives bloom and shine
   In doing good,
   Thou welcome flower
   Of Spring's bright hour,
Sweet lily of the valley!

THE RUNNING STREAM.

I KNOW a beautiful running stream,
  By the green wood-side flowing,
Clear as the sunshine's lucid beam,
  Merrily onwards going;
Over the boulder-stones it leaps,
  And falls in a foamy cascade,
Merrily, merrily onward sweeps
  This stream in beauty arrayed.

In beauty arrayed, this running stream
  Sparkles with light as it's flowing;
Its glittering water is living, I deem,
  And youthful as if it were growing.
Willow and ash, and tremulous aspen,
  Hang down gracefully over its side,
Where clematis and ivy are clasping,
  With fragrant wild roses allied.

Here it crosses the road, this running stream,
  Coming down from the hills with vigorous bound,
And the waggoner stops to freshen his team
  Where water and herbage are found.
Deeper it grows as it travels on
  Into the marsh and over the lea,
Till the running stream and river join,
  And both are lost in the sea.

Wherever it goes, this beautiful stream
   Carries blessings, and leaves them behind ;
And flowers bloom for children's joy, and beam
   In colours of rainbow combined ;
Pastures all verdant smile on its brink,
   Dotted with sheep and with kine,
And the thirsty are welcome to drink,
   And the weary to rest and recline.

There's a moral in this running stream,
   And there's wisdom in its flowing,
And holy thoughts from its waters gleam
   In lessons well worth knowing ;
And the living life which blesses others
   Cheerfully flows on its heavenward road,
And loving all mankind as brothers
   Is the test of our loving God.

MOONLIGHT IN SUMMER.

THE moon is full to-night,
    And though the midnight hour is past,
  There lingers yet some glowing light
    Of sunset in the west.
Creation breathes the deep repose of rest,
While overhead the heavens are clear and vast,
  Sprinkled with only a few bright stars,
The residue eclipsed by the full moon,
  Excepting glorious Mars.
How calm, and cool, and welcome is night's noon,
  After the sultry summer's day !
Fanned by soft zephyrs now, the fevered cheek
Feels the delicious influence of night
  In soothing silence speak,
Inspiring an unspeakable delight
  In spirits pure and meek.

Walk round the garden slowly,
  And take your fill of joy,
This moonlight hour seems holy,
  And free from sin's alloy.
  The light and shade
Of yon high gable roof and Gothic tower
  Are marked with skill artistic and refined ;
These lengthened shadows seem imbued with power
  To elevate the mind.

The gable, with its sacred cross displayed,
The moonlight marks upon the lawn,
And all my thoughts are drawn
    To Calvary's solemn shade.
That cluster of red roses meetly bend
    Over the cross of agony and woe,
And the white roses delicately blend,
    Its sanctity to show.

Now pace this stately avenue of trees,
The moonlight beams are slumbering in the boughs,
    Whose foliage rustles in the passing breeze,
And all the trunks, arranged in shadowy rows,
Seem like cathedral pillars in repose.

Hark ! heard you not the night-hawk scream ?
And whilst upon the old oak's massive root
    We sat, the startled owl, awaking from her dream,
Has flown, and now, with flapping wings
Outspread, repeats her melancholy hoot,
    While on her prey she springs.

The moon has climbed her height,
    And the small hours of morning speed,
While in the east a golden flush
Of rosy hue is colouring to a blush,
    Till dawn succeed,
And the shrill clarion of the farmyard cock
Echoes as true to time as the church clock.

A SUMMER SHOWER.

GLORIOUS summer shower
Of rain for a full hour
Has freshened field and flower,

And the invigorated earth
Smiles gratefully in silent mirth ;
The clouds part, and the sun breaks forth,

To cheer and brighten Nature's face
With youth renewed and sparkling grace,
And give a more elastic pace.

A million drops hang on the trees,
Bejewelled, waving in the breeze,
And on the flowers sweet honey-bees.

The grass revives, and every blade
Is strengthened o'er the vernal glade,
And the parched wild flower lifts its head.

The orchard, laden with rich fruit,
Wakes from its topmost bough to root,
Nourished in its most tender shoot.

The streamlet through the pasture flows
Speedier, and gently overflows
Its banks, to bless where'er it goes.

The full-eared corn drinks in the rain,
Which swells the slowly ripening grain,
And, rustling, scents the verdant plain.

How joyously the feathered throng
Burst into universal song,
Harmonious as a single tongue!

Hedgerow and hawthorn, field and flower,
And village green, and ivied tower,
Look brighter for this summer shower.

Nature's great heart is full of love,
And heaves and throbs new joys to prove,
That human hearts to praise may move.

Oh, let not Nature speak in vain,
But hear and join her grateful strain,—
"God sent us down this summer rain."

OUT IN THE CORN-FIELDS.

OUT in the corn-fields, when the barley bending
   Curves like a sickle with its ripened ears,
And rustles, calling for the harvest tending,
   And harvest-home with cheers.

How the wheat waves with undulating motion
   As the wind gently sways the yielding crop!
Like the calm, beauteous swellings of the ocean
   When breezes rise and drop.

A hundred acres, where the upland fallow
   Was broken up, now smiles in beauty rare;
A hundred acres, full-eared, turning yellow,
   Of ripening wheat is there.

What a sweet scent comes from the corn-lands floating,
   Telling of peace and plenty, love and rest!
O rich aroma! evermore denoting
   A field the Lord has blessed.

Call forth the labourers! scythe and sickle joining,
   O'er the broad fields a thousand hands unite,
Binding the sheaves, and all in songs combining,
   From early morn till night.

Gather the corn in with a loud thanksgiving,
   And praise the Lord with adoration meet,
Who would not thank Him? from His hand receiving
   The finest of the wheat.

OUT IN THE WOODS.

UT in the woods with a bound and a cheer,
Out in the woods while summer is here;
While the midsummer shoot shows it
    delicate green,
Rich foliage above, and bright vistas between.
Tall oaks of the forest and trees of the wood
Stand where for centuries past they have stood,
Waving in glory, and clapping their hands
For joy that they hold a long lease of their lands.
Out in the woods was the place of their birth,
When the acorn was dropped by a rook in the earth;
And there 'mid the storm, and winter's dark moods,
They grew into trees, and spread into woods.

Out in the woods, where the birch and the lime
Cluster like pillars of olden time;
Of wonderful height, and marvellous gauge,
Giants in growth, and hoary with age; •
Their trunks overgrown with ivy and moss,
And their pliable arms stretched across and across.
Tangled and twined and braced overhead,
Only lie down in their bountiful shade

On the green grass, soft as velvet or down.
   Don't you hear the woodpecker tapping above ?
And there leaps the squirrel in mantle of brown,
   And hark ! there's the amorous coo of the dove.

Out in the woods, through brushwood and fern,
And paths that are pathless wherever you turn,
Thistle and briar—only get through !
You will like to gaze on a thirty-mile view.
See, it opens beneath you ! fields, villages, streams,
As if seen from the clouds, or seen in your dreams.
What a vision the eyes take in at a glance !
What landscapes outspread in glorious expanse !
   Sunlight above and sunshine below,
Trains sweeping by in their speed and their might,
   Sails on the river, glittering like snow,
And yonder the dome of St. Paul's is in sight.

Out in the woods ! a service of song,
Out in the woods your anthems prolong,
Nature's cathedral of aspen and birch,
Grand is the nave of the woodland church.
There is the transept, chancel, and aisle,
And pillars of oak in the old Gothic style,
Sacred and solemn.   Birds are the choir,
And the altar-flame is Nature's fire.
Out in the woods is a temple divine,
   Hallowed by prayer and sacred to song ;
Worship the Lord, and bow at His shrine,
   Out in the woods His praises prolong.

Out in the woods are birds of all plumes,
Flowers of all colours, and varied perfumes !
Beautiful grasses, lichen and thyme,
Rose and clematis, and sweet-scented 'Time.'
The pheasant whirrs up from his nest in the "springs,"
And startles you with the rush of his wings.
And the raven floats over you high in the air,
And the hare, and the rabbit, and partridge are there.
Out in the woods, through bushes and brambles,
    Would you feel the full tide of happiness flow ?
Is it health that you seek, and joy in your rambles ?
    Out in the woods, wherever you go.

A SUMMER SUNSET.

A GENTLE wind from the south-west is
      playing
    With the sweet zephyrs in the rustling
      trees,
And now and then the song of peasants haying
    Comes wafted on the breeze.

And overhead the clouds are all entangled
    In wreathing forms of beauty; some are white
And fleecy, others dark, and richly spangled
    With gorgeous hues of light.

In the mid heaven, like snowy mountains piling,
    Alps upon Alps, one over other rose,
While in the distance feathered clouds lay smiling
    In tropical repose.

The sun sinks down, and every cloud is plastic,
    And takes the tinge of glory which he gives;
Short-lived and evanescent, but fantastic,
    Each cloud the stamp receives.

He sinks to rest, between two dark clouds blazing
    In light imperial, brighter than before,
In royal grandeur, terrible, amazing,
    Still glowing more and more.

Brighter and brighter, with intenser lustre,
   The whole horizon glows with living fire;
Strange forms, in endless variation, cluster
     To watch the day expire.

Fainter and fainter, quietly declining,
   Light vanishes, and twilight rules the spheres,
And yonder, like an Eastern diamond shining,
     The evening star appears.

AFTER A DROUGHT.

THE thirsty land is parched, and vegetation
    Droops and turns yellow for the lack of
      rain ;
The sunburnt pastures are a desolation,
    'Midst fields of stunted grain.

The summer streamlets, like the brook at Cherith,
    Of which Elijah drank, are all dried up,
And only prayer to Him who always heareth
    Gives grace and patient hope.

Look toward the sea ! behold, a little cloud
    Rises, no bigger than a human hand ;
Look to the heavens ! behold the sable shroud
    In widening gloom expand.

A hush of silence, as though earth was waiting
    For God to speak in answer to long prayer,
Then a wild lightning flash the clouds inflating,
    And thunder rends the air.

'Tis come at last ! the rain in rich abundance
    Falls, and earth opens her capacious breast ;
The streamlets flow again in God's redundance,
    And sing with bounty blest.

Oh, how the meadows freshen into greenness ;
   And the scorched corn uplifts the opening ear ;
And famished kine, like Pharaoh's for their leanness,
    Low, because rain is here !

The birds, long mute, sing while the rain is falling,
   Warbling their thanks in sweetly varied lays ;
The cheerful skylark upward mounts, forestalling
    Men's hymns in gentle praise.

But now the clouds are breaking, and bright glances
   Of sunshine burst upon the earth again ;
The sunshine is God's smile, and this enhances
    Our thanks for this sweet rain.

OUT ON THE OCEAN.

UT on the ocean, in a trim-built vessel,
   Skimming like sea-bird with its wings
      outspread,
  Before the gale, or lying to, to nestle
    In the waves' bed.

Out on the ocean, when a stiff sou'-wester
  Springs up and drives us from the shore away ;
On flies our tiny bark—and rough winds test her—
    Covered with spray.

Soon the wind drops, and then we turn the rudder,
  And steering shorewards, breast the rolling sea,
And our small ship speeds onwards—a brave scudder,
    Swift, sure, and free.

Some porpoises are rising just before us,
  And shoals of mackerel waiting for the net ;
That listless flock of gulls now floating o'er us
    Seem a dull set.

Sunshine and shadow, in rich variation
  Of beauty exquisite, and ever new,
Play on the waves in soft illumination
    And rainbow hue.

Beating the Channel, hazy in the distance
   A giant steamship plies with mighty stroke,
But seems a speck—the proof of its existence
     A mile of smoke.

But the storm gathers! mingled fear and wonder
   Affright us as we sail; the cliffs in sight,
Clouds thicken, lightning flashes, and the thunder
     Rolls on in might:

Terror and glory wonderfully blending,
   Darkness and light asserting rival sway,
In cloud, and storm, and fiery wrath contending,
     Set in array.

Leaping the foaming billows, buoyant, bounding,
   We cross the sand-bar with a heart elate,
And safely mooring, in the harbour grounding,
     Our joy is great.

MOONLIGHT IN AUTUMN.

THIS is the harvest moon, the yearly sign
  Of providence Divine:
 Seedtime and harvest over hill and vale
 Fail not to come, nor ever shall they fail.
The full-orbed moon is rising in her might,
And men might harvest in her bounteous light.
  The air is mild and calm,
  Breathing delicious balm,
The fragrance of a thousand fields of corn,
 And luscious fruits now ripe, and orchards fair,
Mixed with the odours of autumnal bloom.
Plenty has emptied her full horn,
 And now man's labour and long care
End in the joyous shouts of harvest-home.

The moon looks down with bright benignant smile,
 As though she shared the bounty man receives;
 How vast the gain of toil!
 How wide the range of sheaves!
Dotting the uplands, o'er the valleys spread,
 And crowning the hill-tops!
From heaven God sends us wheaten bread;
 And still the manna drops,
In plentiful supply, down from above,
That men may live, and God His children love.

But see ! black clouds are gathering in the sky,
   The moon is veiled in darkness, and the wind
Rises into a gale.   A storm is nigh !
And now along the horizon a wild flash
   Of lightning blazes, followed close behind
   By a loud thunder-crash ;
   And then a sudden rain,—
Sudden, but short, for soon the clouds disperse,
   And moonlight smiles again,—
Moonlight more beautiful than poet's verse.

   The storm has cleared the air,
And freshened Nature, parched with lengthened drought,
   Owns her Creator's care.
'Tis twilight, and the eyes of morning greet
   The opening day :
The harvesters are waking, and their feet
   Plod on their early way ;
The thrush is singing to the morning star,
   And soon his echoing song will wake the lark ;
I hear the peasant's whistle, and afar
   The faithful watch-dog's bark.

UP ON THE HILLS.

UP on the hills in summer-time,
Up on the hills at morning's prime;
Just as the eastern skies grow bright,
And lingering stars are quenched in light;
Up with a heart gladsome and blithe,
Up with a step healthful and lithe,
Higher and higher, nor linger or stop,
Higher and higher, climb to the top.
Up on the hills at morning's prime,
Up on the hills in summer-time!

Up on the hills, what glories unfold!
The heavens are on fire in crimson and gold.
'Tis sunrise! stand still in awe and amaze;
There's a charm in the warmth of the sun's early rays,
He comes in his grandeur, he comes in his might,
The life-giving power—the centre of light.
The mist rolls away in the valley below,
And his glance gives the dewdrop a diamond's glow,
Sparkling by millions in beauty sublime,
Up on the hills at morning's prime.

Up on the hills in summer-time,
Up on the hills at morning's prime,
When the sky is clear and peacefully calm,
And the air is pure, and the breeze is balm,

And the song-birds sing their sweetest and best,
And the lark mounts up with the dew on his breast,
Carolling joys which God has given,
Till he's lost to the sight in the azure of heaven :
Beautiful sounds, heard by those that climb
Up on the hills at morning's prime.

Up on the hills, what see you, I pray,
At morning's prime,—the glory of day?
Rivers and streams, in beauty arrayed,
Bending and winding through pasture and glade ;
Forests and woods in midsummer sheen,
And ivy-clad towers, which spring up between ;
Homesteads and cottages, castles and towns,
The deer in the park, and sheep on the downs :
Oh, how charming the sight in summer-time,
Up on the hills at morning's prime !

Up on the hills, what see you, I pray,
Over the mountains far away?
The cliff in its outline clearly defined,
The fort with its flag unfurled to the wind ;
And the wide, wide sea in sunshine displayed,
And ships with white sails and streamers arrayed,
Bound from Australia or India they come,
And many a heart is throbbing for home.
And yonder the fleet, the pride of our land,
Lying at anchor, silent and grand,—
Silent and grand, ere six o'clock chime,
Up on the hills at morning's prime.

Up on the hills, what wonders unfold
When the heavens are ablaze in crimson and gold!
When fragrance distils from new-wakened flowers,
Like gales which come wafted from spice-laden bowers;
The heavens clear as crystal, the sun in his might,
And earth, sea, and sky in one glory unite.
Though the sceptic may sneer, and the infidel scoff,
The earth is the Lord's, and the fulness thereof.
With songs of thanksgiving His goodness record,
The strength of the hills is the strength of the Lord.
Oh, outstrip the dawn in sweet summer-time,
Up on the hills at morning's prime.

A HOME IN KENT.

INE be a home on some sweet Kentish hill,
    Screened by ancestral oaks from winter's chill ;
    Where the first golden rays of sunrise stream,
    And sunset brightens with its latest beam !
Blessed with a rich variety of view,—
The calm clear river, all in silvery sheen,
Running with noiseless motion through the vale ;
    The church in sight, with ever-verdant yew,
And lichen-gate with ivy ever green.
Ye happy homesteads, and broad orchards, hail !
The cheerful windmill, and the fields of corn,
    And fragrant hop with aromatic scent !
Here would I live, and die where I was born,
    On some sequestered hill in lovely Kent.

SUNDAY AFTERNOON IN THE COUNTRY.

IT down upon this bank. Those chiming bells
    Are sweet, and sanctify the fragrant breeze
    With a calm Sabbath quiet. Through the dells,
    By varied paths divergent 'twixt the trees,
Or slanting o'er the fields, the peasants come
    To worship God. Cheerful but serious, they
Converse in tones subdued. A healthful bloom
Glows on the cheek of youth. Some aged stoop
Beneath the weight of years. A buoyant group
    Of joyous children, singing " Happy Day,"
Trip through the meadows toward the old church gate.
    And now the pastor comes, his flock to feed
With heavenly bread, and lead them, while they wait
    On God, and meekly ask the blessings which they need.

BEFORE A STORM.

THE air is sultry, and the shrouded sun
  Shines dimly through a veil of misty haze
  With heat oppressive, and where'er we gaze,
We see storm signals, though we may not shun
The coming tempest, with its awful blaze.
The birds sit silent on the leafless boughs,
  And clustering cattle gather in the field,
As if in fear ; while earth's pulsation grows
  Feebler and feebler, all in silence sealed,
Slumbering in deep but dangerous repose.
  Black clouds come rolling up against the wind,
And, meeting darker masses in mid heaven,
  The fire outflashes first, and close behind
The awful thunder bursts, as though the skies were riven.

AUTUMN.

FIELD flowers and summer minstrelsy, farewell!
  The rose is colourless, and fading fast ;
  The choiring birds forget their songs to swell,
  And summer's rich variety is past.
The sere leaves wander, and the hoar of age
  Gathers a trophy for the dying year,
And, following in her quiet pilgrimage,
  Waters her couch with many a pearly tear.
Yet is there one unchanging friend who stays
  To cheer the passage into winter's gloom :—
The redbreast chants his solitary lays,
  A simple requiem over Nature's tomb.
The sweet solemnity of autumn smiles,
And gathered harvests care and fear beguiles.

A MILD DAY IN WINTER.

WHEN the sun rose this morning, his
  first glances
    Were warm and genial as the breath of
      Spring !
And as he climbs the sky, and day advances,
    The birds begin to sing.

The skylark, rising with uncertain flight,
  And shyly warbling, sings, but swiftly drops ;
And yonder thrush swells forth his new delight
    Down in the alder copse.

'Tis but mid-January, yet the south banks
  Are green ; and violets peeping here and there,
And snowdrops in their variegated ranks
    By the warm hedge appear.

The lilac buds are swelling, and the limes
  Tinged with red hues ; and o'er my study shade
Sparrows are chirping of the pleasant times
    When matches shall be made.

And o'er the meadows there's a sign of waking,
  And tender grass shoots up amid the gloom ;
And here behold !—sure sign of Winter's breaking—
    A daisy in full bloom.

A few more tempests, and perhaps deep snowing—
  Some frosts in February, then a thaw,—
And Spring shall come, with May-day garlands blowing,
    Bright as e'er poet saw.

THE WINTER RIVULET.

FROST and snow
    Where'er I go,
  Rivers, streams and brooks
    Bound in chains,
    Hills, moors, and plains,
  And Nature's rural nooks.

  Winter reigns,
  And farmers' wains,
Harrow, plough, and drill,
  Cannot stir,
  So the loud whirr
Of daily life is still.

  Not a sound
  Is heard around.
Yes ! one small voice I hear,
  One sweet song
  All winter long,
In accents soft and clear.

  Frost and snow
  May come and go,
Rivers bind and lakes,
  But they forget
  This rivulet
Which summer music makes.

Storms may beat,
And cold or heat,
December come, or June,
Chanting still,
This living rill
Is never out of tune.

When no bird
Of song is heard,
And trees are stark and bare,
Woods snow-crowned
And pools ice-bound,
The merry rill is there.

Day and night,
In pure delight,
To loving music set,
Sung alone,
Thy hymn goes on,
Thou woodland rivulet.

WINTER BY THE SEA-SHORE.

HE curving shore is fringed with ice and snow
    Far as the eye can reach—in frozen blocks,
And thousands of wild sea-birds come and go
    In countless flocks.

Some paddling on the icebergs, and some flying,
    In form triangular and number vast ;
While the swift oxbirds, all in speed outvying,
    Go sweeping past.

Plovers and ducks, and wild geese in abundance,
    Hover o'erhead, or settle on the sea ;
God sends them in such plentiful redundance
    For all men free.

But hark ! a shot with sharp reverberation
    Re-echoes loudly from a fowler's boat ;
And the shrill shriek of fear and consternation
    Alarm denote.

For that one shot, with well-directed aim,
    Swept lengthwise through a hundred wings outspread,
And over twenty of the ocean game
    Fall maimed or dead.

But evening comes, and o'er the darkening skies
   In moving clouds the affrighted birds retreat,
Just as the full moon's earliest beams arise
     Serenely sweet.

The rising tide comes moaning toward the beach,
   Lifting the crisp ice with a measured flow.
Beautiful sea! as far as eye can reach
     Belted with snow.

SHOTTENDEN MILL.

(NEAR CANTERBURY.)

N the top of a hill
    Stands Shottenden Mill;
    And whenever the breeze is blowing
    The sails swing round,
  And the corn is ground,
And the mill is always going.
Round and round, with hearty good-will,
Sweep the sails of Shottenden Mill.

    All the year round
    Corn must be ground,
For God sends bread for the eater;
    So there's no standing still
    At Shottenden Mill.
Round and round, fleeter and fleeter,
Merrily swing the sails of the mill
On the top of Shottenden Hill.

    Sunshine or mist,
    There's always a grist
To grind, or for man or for beast;

Light winds or strong,
Short days or long,
Never from labour released.
Round and round, with a whirr of good-will,
Swing the sails of Shottenden Mill.

This hard-working mill
On the top of the hill
Is oak-braced with many a rivet;
And it braves the wild storm's
Most terrible forms,
And long may it stand to outlive it.
Hurricanes fierce have swept over the hill,
But firm as a rock stands Shottenden Mill.

And sailors see
This mill out at sea,
And a welcome beacon it stands
Their passage to guide
Until they outride
The tempest and Goodwin Sands.
Brave hearts, steering with courage and skill
By this beacon sign on Shottenden Hill.

In the olden day,
The book-learnèd say,
On this hill was Cæsar's camp;
But now they grind corn
Where the blast of the horn
Was heard, and the Romans' tramp.
And the country smiles in peace and good-will,
And plenty of wheat at Shottenden Mill.

Round and round,
With a humming sound,
Go the sails by night and by day ;
And the grists are sent
Till the stock is spent,
And the flour is carried away.
And round and round go the sails of the mill
Which stands on the top of Shottenden Hill.

MOONLIGHT IN WINTER.

THE winter moon shines clearly,
    And the stars like diamonds bright,
  And the frost bites severely
    On this December night.
Deep lies the snow upon the ground ;
  Its frozen surface, yielding to my feet,
Breaks with a sharp, crisp sound,
  Which echoes oft repeat.

Stand still !   The silence is intense ;
  No sound is heard
From sky, or landscape stretching out immense,
  From man, or beast, or bird.
It seems as though Creation's pulse had stopped,
  And all mankind had fled,
And earth in a white winding-sheet were wrapped,
  And that all life was dead.

Look round and see,—
  What is there else than snow ?
Fields, woods, hills, valleys, upland, marsh, or lea,
  Glittering in moonlight glow.
  Nothing but snow, snow, snow !
In some primeval forest, before man,
  Or beasts, or birds were made,
Or God His six days' work began,
  Perchance such death-like silence might pervade.

But men *are* living still.
I hear a sound of music from the hill,—
Sweet music like unto the angels' song,
 Peace and good-will on earth ;
So the young villagers do now prolong
 That burst of heavenly mirth.

Sweet is their melody, made doubly sweet
Because the Babe of Bethlehem they greet.
A Christmas carol, like a voice from heaven,
Proclaims God reconciled, and man forgiven.
Was ever silence broken more sublimely,
Or midnight hymn more welcome or more timely ?

The moon looks mildly down to earth,
 And one star, like a pure celestial gem,
Shines on the church's cross, as at His birth
 Christ's star shone over Bethlehem.
The midnight bells a peal are ringing,
 And softly the pale moonbeams play ;
So Christmas eve, 'mid joyous singing,
 Gives place to Christmas day.

THE CHRISTMAS GORSE.

WELCOME is the cheerful gorse,
Lighting up the moor and moss,
In dark winter's misty gloom
Beaming out in brilliant bloom;
All its thorny boughs are green,
Bright with golden flowers between;
Never looks the gorse more gay
Than it smiles on Christmas day.

Lingering by this wayside brook,
Take a little closer look;
Watered as the streamlet flows,
Here it flourishes and grows;
Delving downwards with its roots,
Upwards spring its vigorous shoots.
See the gorse in full array,
Blossoming on Christmas day.

Never in the vernal spring,
With its variegated wing,
When the nightingale and thrush
Sing in every brake and bush,—
Never do we prize the flowers
As in winter's stormy hours.
Beauteous gorse! like radiant May,
Garlanded on Christmas day.

Welcome, then, the yellow gorse
On the common, moor, and moss ;
On the upland, in the field,
Clumped along the marsh and weald.
Blooming gorse, I'll take of thee
Branches for my Christmas-tree ;
And on Jesu's cradle lay
Golden flowers on Christmas day.

ON A SNOWY MORNING.

THE morning breaks with more than Sabbath
stillness,
And all the roads are blocked with drifted
snow ;
And we all seem to share the general chillness,
For none can come or go.

The trees are snow-clad, with their arms extended,
And yonder some long boughs, o'erburdened, break ;
Yet while men slept, this ponderous mass descended
In silence, flake by flake.

And hill and valley, robed in virgin whiteness,
Glisten beneath the wintry sunbeam's smile ;
Emblem of purity and moral brightness
In hearts that know no guile.

By whirlwinds driven, or breezes' gentler breathing,
Wrought with artistic beauty without toil,
Arches and columns rise, and foliage wreathing
Like some cathedral aisle.

Alcoves, all interlaced with creeping briar
And wild geranium, roofing fairy bowers ;
And trees entwined with blossoms, climbing higher,
All rich with snowy flowers.

The noisy rooks in flight to-day are still,
   And find nor field nor upland without snow ;
While the pert robin chirps upon the sill,
     "Your charity bestow."

But hark ! a shout comes ringing o'er the knoll,—
   A hundred schoolboys, with tumultuous roar
And merry laughter, all united, roll
     A snowball to my door.

Rosy and healthful children, full of glee !
   The frozen mass resists their further pains ;
The mighty snowball under an old tree
     Immoveable remains.

FUGITIVE THOUGHTS ABOUT BIRDS.

THE WOODCOCK.

THE lonely woodcock, solitary bird,
    Takes wing when others sleep ;
Just after sunset, and between the lights,
    He seeks some silent copse or murmuring
        stream,
    With swift, uneven flight.
Down in the marshy dyke, 'midst sedge and flags,
He loves to wander, hermit-like, alone.
When the frost binds the earth, and snow lies deep,
The woodcock is where the clear rivulet flows
Unbound by icy chains, and there in peace
He finds content and food while others starve.
Bird of bright eye and plumage beautiful,
The sportsman's prize and epicure's delight.

THE SNIPE.

BIRD of swift wing, but short and wavy flight,
Coming with winter's earliest storm, and gone
Before the primrose blows.   Rising with a scream
Of shrill affright.   Thy haunt is by the brook,
Which sings meandering through the lonely wood,
Or in the reedy vale.   Suddenly rising,
After brief flight thou dost as sudden fall,
Again to wade the streamlet in its course.

'Tis said a snipe found sport for one long season
For an old gentleman who loved the field,
Who fired away from Michaelmas till March,
But never bagged his game.
                          The snipe escaped unhurt,
And snipe and sportsman were alike content.

THE THRUSH.

THE thrush is the most musical of birds,
Quite prodigal of song.   The wintry day
Is often cheered by his melodious notes,
When from the leafless branches of the ash
He pours out harmony from morn till eve,
And in the summer season sings till Night
Has lit her constellations of bright stars.

THE HERON.

HARK! overhead I hear the heron's call,
Who, high in air, defies the fowler's gun.
Bird of broad wings, and lengthened neck and beak,
Who, flying slowly, seeks the sea-side dyke,
And ever and anon repeats his cry,
Till, after sunset, in the evening's dusk,
He turns towards his lonely heronry,
Built in some aristocracy of trees,
Planted in feudal days, and centuries old,
And carrying with him now a goodly fish
To serve the night's repast.

THE CUCKOO AND THE NIGHTINGALE.

THE cuckoo and the nightingale, they say,
Come on their visit on the selfsame day :
One sings in sweet monotony by day,
The other cheers the night with melting lay :
One flies and publishes the news of spring,
And, never tiring, spreads his fluttering wing ;
The other, in lone wood or sylvan copse,
Sings till the spangled dew of morning drops,
From sunset till the stars are quenched in light ;
And then the cuckoo sings from morn till night.
Sweet birds of passage.   When the weeks of spring
Are past, both stretch again the silent wing,
And fly, no one knows whither, for a while,
To come again when spring again shall smile.

ROOKS IN THE SNOW.

IN a deep snow, a rookery assembled,
Perched on some towering oaks and spreading elms,
To hold a conference of collective wisdom
On the great question of their daily food.
Much cawing was there, and the long debate
At length grew noisy—many spoke at once.
Then rounds of cawing followed ; till at length
There came a silence, broken now and then
By one or two, who settled the debate.
A deputation of two ancient rooks
Flew seawards toward the marshes, as though sent
To spy the country and bring back the news.
Now for a while a solemn silence reigned,

And not a member left his proper perch
Until the two commissioners returned
And brought a good report.   Three times they cawed,
Equivalent to three times three in cheers ;
Then the whole flock took flight, and with hoarse rounds
Of loud applause, flew downwards to the marsh.

ROOKS IN SPRING (A SONNET).

EARLY in spring the rooks begin to build,
And wake the frozen echoes of the glade
With their uproarious noise.   The ear is filled
From morning's dawn till nightfall, and their trade
Seems brisker than the town or market field.
All are at work, and yonder row of limes
Furnishes timber without leave or cost ;
Each twists his twig, and comes a hundred times
To the same tree.   Identity is lost
Among so many thousands of one hue,
Yet still each couple know their rightful nest,
And all good rooks are to each other true.
The farmer's friends are rooks, or else the pest
Of grub would eat their corn, and blight destroy the rest.

A FLIGHT OF STARLINGS.

DOWN in the marshes, nigh unto the sea,
Walking one wintry day, I heard a sound
O'erhead, which startled me with fear,
And looking up, beheld a flight of birds,
In numbers past computing—like a cloud,
Moving in one dark mass towards the south,

Swift as the fowler's dart—compact and one,
As though I only saw a single bird.
The air was stirred to motion, and the rush
Of wings innumerable was sublime ;
Ezekiel's vision flashed across my mind,
And the loud rustle of a thousand wings
Of angels, flying on some high behest ;
One will, one speed, one common haven in view,
With pace unflagging, they their flight pursue.
Millions of starlings ! sweeping through the skies,
May teach a lesson men should not despise ;
Guided by instinct, and a Hand divine,
They all unite and answer God's design.

THE JACKDAW.

In the grey ivy-mantled Norman tower
Of an old church the jackdaw finds his home ;
And, had we power to understand his talk,
Could tell us of an ancestry renowned,
And long remembered in the jackdaw world ;
Who dwelt in the same tower for centuries past,
Back to the days of Becket and of Laud ;
Changes have swept, like tempests o'er the land,
But still they hold their own, and none invades
Their freehold, or disputes their ancient right,—
Possession is with them a settled law,
And jackdaws bid defiance to the world.
Perched on the vane, they view the country round,
And after they have made complete survey,
Send forth their foragers afield for food.
For ever happy, whether winter frowns,

Or spring or summer smiles, or autumn glows,
Their tide of joy in even current flows.
The jackdaw code of government is right,
Whoever holds the reins, he holds them tight;
And so, where'er the jackdaw subjects roam,
Content and fed, they dwell in peace at home.

THE HAWK.

On a bright day of sunshine in July,
Veering and swimming in a cloudless sky,
Now swift, now slow, now fixed, with outstretched wings,
A hawk o'erhead is watching for his prey;
Sudden as thought, with lightning speed he springs
To seize a bird which flew across his way:
With swooping flight, his talons and his beak
Prepared (like human hawks) to crush the weak.
But as he pounced upon his frighted foe,
The little bird dropt to the sward below;
While the fierce hawk, in following his fall,
Flew with full force against an ancient wall:
And there I found him, stunned with wings outspread,
And bloody beak and talons, warm, but dead;
While a grey linnet on a neighbouring spray,
Sang, as I deemed, the tyrant's funeral lay.

THE SWALLOW.

How welcome are the swallows, when they come
In early summer, swimming one by one,
Through the blue sky.   Under the straw-thatched eave

We hear again their cheerful twittering voice,
Sound through the casement, and perhaps the same
Sweet birds that sung and talked to us last year.
To me they are like long-lost friends come back,
To see the faces and the home they love ;
And as the children laugh and sing within,
Their buoyant chirp commingles, and they seem
Part of the family in love and joy.
Securely, under the o'erhanging roof
They build and hatch, and feed and fledge their young ;
And often peeping from their plastered house,
They look into our window without fear,
And chirp as though they said, " Our home is here."
And sometimes in an undertone they sing,
Softly as the clear melody of streams ;
But when the early glooms of autumn come,
Again they migrate to a warmer home.

THE CUCKOO.

THE cuckoo sings all through the cloudiest day,
And heeds not though the bitter east wind blow,
And rain descends ; herself for ever joyous,
She tells her joy, that others may be glad.
In storm or sunshine still she sings the same
Short, cheerful tune, and spreads her jubilant wing
To sound her welcome to approaching spring.
The weeping child, the moment that he hears
Her voice, cries—" cuckoo," and dries up his tears ;
The aged greet her, and affliction's cheek
Is flushed with sudden joy, to hear the cuckoo speak.

Part Three.—Miscellaneous Poems.

THE MAIL TRAIN.

FROM the siding slowly gliding,
　　Almost sleeping, gently creeping,
　　　　Comes the engine towards the line—
　　Brightly polished brasses gleaming,
Blazing fire and vapour steaming
For the mighty work combine.

See the stalwart driver stand
With his hand upon the mane
Of his tireless flaming steed,
Guiding his speed
At his own will or need
To stop, or run, or fly.
How calmly resolute and grand
He looks while passing by,
And followed by the train.

A noble engine, high in fame,
The "Wellington"—a deathless name,—
And high in speed and mighty power
To cover fifty miles an hour.

The carriages are first and second,
Fourteen together reckoned.
Beside the luggage-van and tender,
And horse-box carrying racers,
(Lord Derby's swiftest pacers!)
But oh! what beauty, wealth, and splendour,
Comes crowding forth
From east and west, from south and north.
Squires, merchants, bishops, farmers, traders,
And Ethiopian serenaders.
The bounding young, all joy and glee,
Sweet laughing children blithe and free ;
And tremulous old, and rich and poor,
All hurrying to the carriage door.
The train is full—five hundred souls
Are packed together there ;
The whistle sounds, away it rolls,
And leaves the platform bare.

With watchful heed, but rising speed,
The iron horse pursues his course !
The eagle eye and steady hand
That drives can regulate the force
And hold him in command.
The city lights grow dim and few,
And vanish from the sight
In deep dark night,
And only leave in view
Two flaming eyes before
A rush of something undefined,
Which passes with a thunder-roar,
And two red stars behind !

Onwards ! like a meteor flashing,
Gathering speed—gathering speed ;
Under bridges, over ridges,
Onwards ! blazing, hissing, dashing,
Terrible indeed !
Past the solitary station,
Quick as thought—it comes—'tis gone—
O'er the giddy elevation,
O'er the viaduct of stone,
Flaming on—alone—alone !
See below—nay, do not quiver !
Underneath us runs a river,
Making melancholy moan,
Flowing on—flowing on.
See ! a ship is sailing under ;
On we sweep ! on we sweep !
As though we cleared it with a leap,
In fear and wonder.
But hark ! a sound like thunder
Bursts with electric shock,
Or blast of granite rock,
The whistle's shrill and startling sound
Tells us we are underground,
In a tunnel three miles long.
On we fly ! on we fly !
Our charger never was so strong,
Or speed so high ;
Without slackening or strain
He springs into fresh air again.

Onward sweeping—onward sweeping,
While the silent world is sleeping.

Onward sweeping—onward sweeping,
With a flare of lurid glare;
Never weary, though the dreary
Midnight chills the air.
Alps of chalk on either hand,
Then through Apennines of sand;
Iron bridges hung on chains,
Where mountain spasms
Have left wide chasms.
Giant tubes—through which the trains
Travel by the light of gas.
Still our never-flagging horse
Shoots on his lightning course!
So, falling back with folded arms,
Over our eyes we draw our cap,
To take a gentle nap
Oblivious of alarms.

   *   *   *   *   *

What's the shaking? are we waking?
Can we have slept on an hour?
What a screech the whistle's making!
Every break puts on its power,
We have slept for many an hour.
Sweetly waking—morning's breaking,
Summer morning's primest hour;
Yonder is our journey's end,
Yonder is the glorious sea;
Softly round the curve we bend,
Slow and easy as may be;
Spires all glittering in light,
Noble cliffs and sweeping bays
Burst all bright upon the sight.

Friendly meetings—happy greetings—
Loving bands all shaking hands;
Crowds of fathers, brothers, cousins,
Uncles, aunts, and lovers—dozens !
Groups of friends already come,
Welcome everybody home.

Gently from the platform gliding,
See the conquering engine go ;
Put him back upon the siding,
Quench his fiery heart, and blow
Off the steam ; and let him dream,
Hazily and lazily.
On that siding still abiding,
In a deep, unconscious sleep,
There a holiday to keep
Until duty's call shall come,
See " The Wellington " at home !

THE PATRIOT'S SONG.

HILE empires rise and despots fall,
And kingdoms pass away,
Old England soars above them all,
In proud imperial sway.
A patriot monarch on her throne,
Her bulwarks on the sea,
She stands invincible, alone,
Old England shall be free.

Whatever coward nations fear
  Of tyranny and wrong,
Immortal liberty is here,
  The vaunt of every tongue.
Our native land is freedom's seat,
  Ordained by Heaven's decree ;
Wherever slavery may retreat,
  Old England shall be free.

The British lion calmly stands ;
  Should hostile hordes attack,
A million loyal hearts and hands
  Would rush to drive them back.
Britannia, with unruffled brow,
  Still holds the scales of right,
In majesty that will not bow,
  And consciousness of might.

Ours is a land of noble hearts,
  A land of noble deeds ;
Where loving charity imparts
  To every one that needs.
Where royal might and right are joined,
  And tyrants are unknown ;
And love and kind affections bind
  The cottage to the throne.

Old England ! never shall her shore
  By foreign foe be trod ;
She grasps her arms as heretofore,
  And puts her trust in God.

While hearts of oak her rights defend,
  Brave hearts by land and sea,
And Liberty is England's friend,
  Old England shall be free.

Her glorious fleets upon the wave,
  Her ramparts on the shore ;
Her sons, the children of the brave,
  Who crushed their foes of yore.
Where'er the British flag's unfurled,
  Her sovereignty we see ;
Hurrah ! in spite of all the world,
  Old England shall be free.

THE VOICE OF THE OLD YEAR.

RING out the old year's wonders,
    With things all past and gone ;
  The battle with its thunders,
    And conflicts lost and won :
Where the hostile hosts assembled,
  To the bloody combat led ;
And the earth, the old earth, trembled
  Beneath their giant tread.
Where the angry foemen crowded,
  As foot to foot they stood ;
And thousands fell enshrouded
  In winding-sheets of blood.

Ring out the old year's wonders,
   And let war for ever cease,
And no more be heard its thunders ;
   And ring in the reign of peace.

Ring out the old year's records
   Of violence and wrongs ;
The two-edged swords of bitter words,
   Brandished by wicked tongues.
Oppression with its hateful deeds,
Done to the widow in her weeds ;
And fraud and falsehood deep and black,
   And the strong trampling down the weak ;
And midnight murderers on the track
   Of victims whom they seek ;
And secret sins, and public shame,
   And Sabbath days defiled ;
And God's own word unread, unheard,
   And mercy's offers mild
Flung back to heaven from whence they came,
   And repentance still deferred.
O biting memories of the past !
   O solemn closing year !
Well may a nation stand aghast
   In agony and fear !
And just before the old year dies
   Confess her sins,
And lift to heaven her suppliant eyes
   Ere the new year begins.
Oh, ring out the old year's crimes,
   To be done no more—no more ;

And ring in, ye new year's chimes,
Good words, good deeds, good times
  For evermore.

Ring out the old year's evil,
The world, the flesh, the devil;
  Let them go! let them go!
And ring in the days of love,
And the Pentecostal Dove,
  And paradise below.
When not a slave the whole earth round
Shall tread on God's free ground;
But liberty in stalwart youth
Walk hand in hand with truth.

Then ring out the old year's evil,
The world, the flesh, the devil;
  Let them go! let them go!
And ring in the Prince of Peace,
  Messiah's gentle reign.
And let war and bloodshed cease,
  And righteousness obtain.
Ring, ring out the old year's crimes,
  And ring in the new year's birth,—
Good words, good deeds, good times;
Oh, were ever sweeter chimes
  Rung on this fallen earth
Since creation's virgin anthem rang,
And morning stars together sang?

THE GREAT WESTERN EXPRESS.

N we go, on we go,
    With tremendous power,
    Always would we travel so—
    Fifty miles an hour.
Free from oscillation,
    Swift and sure endeavour
To fly past every station.
    Broad gauge for ever !

On we go, on we go,
    Quietly reclining ;
Express cannot stop, you know,
    So do not think of dining.
Open *Telegraph* or *Times*,
    Con the sparkling leader,
Or (if a nap you want) the rhymes
    Which send to sleep the reader.

You'd like to view the scenery—
    Look sharp ! and mount your glasses,—
Brick-making, steam machinery,
    A farmhouse, sheep, and asses.
That's a river we flew over,
    With boats lying at the ferry,
And that's a field of clover—
    We are travelling fast ! oh, very !

Half a dozen ploughs
   Working in one field,
Just as many cows
   Grazing in the weald ;
Two sportsmen with retrievers
   For partridges are touting ;
See ! those labourers wave their beavers—
   How lustily they're shouting !

There's the town of Reading,
   Passed before you look ;
See the sunshine shedding
   Diamonds on the brook.
That's a splendid church
   Towering o'er the woodland,
And a school beneath a birch,—
   This ought to be a good land.

On we go, on we go,
   A mile of vapour steaming ;
Now and then a little slow,
   While the whistle's screaming,
"Clear the line for the express !"
   Every signal dropping
Says, "All right !"—they can't say less,
   We cannot think of stopping.

Yonder's Bath and Clifton,
   That is Kingswood School ;
Oh, don't we get swift on ?
   And yet so calm and cool.

There is Bristol with its towers,
   Grand Redcliff, and the river ;
Down from London in two hours—
   Broad gauge for ever !

On we go, on we go,—
   Great Western speed is glorious ;
Honour to Brunel and Co.,
   And Stephenson victorious !
Always sure—never frightening—
   What a bold endeavour
To overtake the lightning !
   Broad gauge for ever !

STARS.

BEAUTIFUL stars ! nought shadows or
     mars
    Your exquisite light,
Which shines as it shone on Eden's birth-
     night ;
In radiance of love, looking down from above,
   With tremulous smile,
As though ye were seeking for hearts without guile.

O wonderful stars ! 'mid earthquakes, and wars,
   And desolate thrones,
Unscathed in unapproachable zones.
Some strong in their might, like lightnings in flight
   Through infinite space ;
Some fixed where they hang, and eternally blaze.

Oh, speak to me, stars ! Saturn, Jupiter, Mars,
     And tell of your birth,
Of warfare in heaven, and the founding of earth.
Sing over again that rapturous strain
     Which rang through the sky
When angels and stars were shouting for joy.

Say, primitive stars, saw ye ocean's strong bars
     By Omnipotence rent,
When land, sea and sky in the Deluge were blent ;
And the ark floated on, as ye quietly shone
     O'er the turbulent flood,
Engulfing a world at the fiat of God ?

When Bethlehem's star brought light from afar,
     And Jesus was born,
While angels were singing from midnight till morn,
Did ye shine on that night ? or, veiling your light,
     In silence behold
Heaven's wonder of love in the Infant unfold ?

Oh, tell me, pure stars, when in anguish and scars
     He hung on the tree,
Looked ye earthwards that sorrowful sight to see ?
If in dread and amaze the sun hid his face,
     Ye sympathized too,
Till a curtain of clouds hid the scene from your view.

Tell me, calm, placid stars, how the fiery-wheeled cars
     Of comets sweep on,
Waving sceptres of flame on their terrible throne.
Are they monarchs who reign, or rebels unslain
     Who in conflict delight,
And challenge celestial armies to fight ?

O millions of stars ! no schisms or jars
    Ever ruffled your peace ;
Submissive to law, ye seek no release ;
But gentle and clear shine each in your sphere,
    Obedient to God,
Contented to dwell in your royal abode.

O beautiful stars ! nought shadows or mars
    Your diamond light,
Nor rust or decay makes your lustre less bright ;
In numbers unknown ye look smilingly down
    From your palace above,
And silently tell your story of love.

DOWN AT THE SEA-SIDE.

DOWN at the sea-side, at Margate or Dover,
    Escaped from the smoke and worry of
        town,
    Paterfamilias again is a rover,
        Longing again on the sands to lie down.
Whirled by the rail, himself and his spouse,
  With six boys and girls, and Phœbe the maid,
Seek solace awhile at Adelaide House,
  Glad of green fields, with sunshine and shade.

How the current of joy increases its speed !
  The pulse that was sluggish grows active once more.
Soon is the step lithe as the deer in the mead ;
  And the children are bounding along the sea-shore,

Cheerful and happy—the family group
  Sketching and reading, or climbing the height,—
Dressing the doll or trundling the hoop,
  Shouting in glee and childish delight.

Down on the beach, when the tide is retiring,
  And fishermen mending their nets on the sands,
Juvenile navvies, to fortune aspiring,
  Scoop out their tunnels, and stake out their lands.
Viaducts, cuttings, and sometimes a station,
  Is speedily made with labour and pains;
But their contracts turn out a bad speculation,—
  Swept by the tide, not a vestige remains.

Isn't it charming to lie down on the sands,
  Tossing the pebbles or counting the sails !
When children's loud laugh, or clapping of hands,
  Echoes like music afloat on the gales.
Up on the cliff's outer edge is a cow,
  Chewing her cud in silent content,
Looking towards France, and making a bow,
  As if thanks for the treaty of commerce was meant.

Then a trip by the train to Folkestone or Hythe,—
  Rich are the hills, the valleys are sweet,
And in hay-time or harvest the swoop of the scythe
  Falls on the ear in some rural retreat.
Binding the sheaves of barley or wheat,
  The sinewy labourers, embrowned by the sun,
Cheerfully work, nor shrink from the heat,
  Until the harvest supper is won.

R

Beautiful ocean ! bright are thy waves,
   Glittering beneath the smile of the moon.
Terrible ocean ! when the storm raves,
   Dashing in fury from midnight till noon,
Surging and heaving like mountains and hills,
   Loosened and bowed by Omnipotent power,
Crashing and roaring till the heart chills,
   Trembling beneath the thunder-cloud's lour.

Beautiful ocean ! unruffled and calm,
   Kissing the pebbles that lie on the shore
So gently, that none would deem that a qualm
   Could ever disturb thy peace any more.
Lovingly heaves thy motherly breast,
   Hardly moving the skiffs as they lazily float.
Beautiful ocean ! slumbering at rest,
   Rippling as smoothly as river or moat.

Down at the sea-side, dipped in the brine,
   Gathering seaweed or searching for shells,
Whistling the gulls as you idly recline,
   And catching the far-off chiming of bells.
Ruddy and healthful, jocund and gay,
   Paterfamilias joins in the glee ;
Down at the sea-side a month and a day
   With the family group, who so happy as he ?

THE ENGLISHMAN'S SONG.

THE patriot loves his native land,
    A loyal man and true ;
He scorns and shuns the traitor-band ;
    A noble Briton ! See him stand
Beneath his banner blue !
Unmoved amidst the changing scene,
He loves old England and her Queen.

With honest pride he guards her fame,
    And glories in her might ;
The magic power of England's name
Spreads through the world, a beacon flame
    For liberty and right.
The slave that springs upon her shore
Is free, and wears the chain no more.

Old England ! let another boast
    Of lands beyond the sea,
The patriot loves her sea-girt coast—
For ever loves, but loves her most,
    Because her sons are free.
Her flag of liberty unfurled
Waves proudly, master of the world.

Old England gives the poor their bread,
　And takes the outcast in;
By gentle hands the blind are led,
And love kneels down beside the bed
　Of misery and sin.
Soft voices and kind hearts unite
To make affliction's burden light.

Old England is a noble land,
　And makes the youth her care.
She leads the infant by the hand,
And English children understand
　Sweet words of praise and prayer.
Her safeguard is God's word of truth,
Her future hope her rising youth.

Old England is a noble land,
　Her sons are brave and true;
The Saxon dares his foes withstand;
No conqueror invades her strand,
　Where floats the banner blue.
The Briton's badge of freedom there
Is dear as life, but free as air.

Old England, then, with three times three!
　We love our island home;
Where liberty and law agree,—
And bow to law and liberty
　Wherever we may roam.
Her laurels are for ever green,
God save Old England and her Queen!

MIDNIGHT BELLS.

I.—A MUFFLED PEAL FOR THE OLD YEAR.

HE poet rings a muffled peal
    While the old year is dying,
    In sympathy with all that feel
    Deep throbs of bitter anguish steal
Over the memories of the past—
Shadows from some huge sorrow cast
    That set their hearts a-sighing.

Sighing for what? for brothers slain
In war on the Bohemian plain;
For fathers, well last New-Year's day,
Whom death has snatched away;
For loving mothers, in the prime
    Of life and womanhood,
    And daughters beautiful as good;
The grandsire, patriarch of his time,
    And dear old grandmother, who stood
Last year for us to love her,
    Three generations round her there,
The branch of mistletoe above her.
    But now we see the empty chair!
    All gone! and many a hearth is bare
That rang with joy a year ago,
And many a storm-cloud, black and dreary
    Hangs o'er the homestead once so gay;
And thousands moan, in sickness weary,
    Longing for day.

And so the old year dies,
  And so time flies
On to the " rapids " and the mighty " fall,"
Where death and doom await us all.
But hark ! the new year knocks !
  No longer for past sorrows delve,—
Big Ben, St. Paul's, and twenty City clocks
  Strike twelve !

II.—A MERRY PEAL FOR THE NEW YEAR.

THE concert of bells, the beautiful bells !
From thousands of towers in cities and towns,
    In gentle vibrations,
    And sweet undulations,
  And ever-varying modulations,
Now soft and now loud, in passionate swells,
Over the mountains, and valleys, and dells,
  'Mid the city crowd, on the drearisome downs,—
Everywhere bells, musical bells !
On moors and in woodlands, where nobody dwells,
Ringing in concert—old English bells,—
  From ivy-clad belfries in cities and towns,
Ringing together, ringing for joy ;
  Ringing at midnight's silent hour,
Just as though pleasure had no alloy,
  And earth no sin,
So they merrily ring from steeple and tower,
  Thousands of bells, thousands of bells.
One might dream, so glad is the news they bring,

There would never be any more knells,
 Or battle's din,
While they joyously sing, and merrily ring
 The old year out and the new year in.

Ringing for what? for what, I pray,
Should the bells ring on New-Year's day?
For the land that we love, which puts forth her might
For the conquest of wrong and the triumph of right;
For the Queen on her throne, whose sceptre is swayed
 Over millions at home, and millions abroad;—
Mildly she reigns, and her laws are obeyed;
Firmly she rules, and tyrants are awed;
Over the land, or crossing the sea,
Wherever he goes a Briton is free!

So we ring joy-bells for our island home,—
For England, no longer the vassal of Rome;
For the family Bible which lies on the stand,
The charm of our homes and light of our land;
 For our Sabbaths, calm, peaceful, and sweet,
With their whispers of love from heaven above,
 And the hallowèd shrines where households meet,
Under the wings of the holy Dove,
And festive groups, and kindly meetings,
New-Year's gifts and friendly greetings,
Hands grasped, long severed, reunited,
And lamps of youthful love fresh lighted;
And children dancing in their glee
Around the Christmas-tree;
 The prodigal come home again,
And bowing at his father's knee,
 His pardon to obtain.

That's why the bells so merrily ring,
  The prodigal son is forgiven;
And an angel spreads his snowy wing,
  And carries the news to heaven.

But the bells suddenly cease,
And all is peace—all is peace.
Over the landscape silence reigns,
Deep, solemn silence, like the still of death,
As though earth held her breath;
Or drew, with mighty inspiration,
Life in a new creation.
And on the threshold of the opening year
  Stands Time, unwrinkled, and with look serene,
Upon his brow, nor smile nor frown appear;
  But with grave gaze he views the mingled scene
In pondering thought, and lest the festive chimes
  Should make us all too blithe,
Behold him stop our music and our rhymes,
  Sharpening his scythe.

London. J. & W. Rider, Printers, 14, Bartholomew Close, E.C.